The Great Atlantic Highway

& Other Stories

PRAISE FOR THE GREAT ATLANTIC HIGHWAY

"Steve Gergley's stories are funny, sinister, and disorientingly off-kilter. Taken as a whole, this book creates an immersive and haunting world of its own, a shadow that will follow you for long after you've finished the book."

—Dan Chaon, author of *Among the Missing* and *Stay Awake*

"From Gergley's vast breadth of imagination comes a new collection of nearly 50 short stories. Some are a dozen pages long, while others are under 500 words. Through this hyperactive, humorous, and horrifying display, we see human statues, ruthless gods, impossible bridges, and Schwarzenegger chat rooms. We see a soldier falling from the sky and a window inside of a tooth. Vengeful murder, bears, actors, and apples. Hardcore vs. death metal. A blurring between video game and dream. A modernist approach with a biblical gaze. It all takes place inside a brutalist society atop a brutalist planet so the magic that (frequently) happens is splattered in grit. Opening this book feels like visiting a drug dealer in an abandoned mall. Pocket a lighter. Bring a knife."

—Ben Niespodziany, author of *No Farther than the End of the Street* and *Cardboard Clouds*

"Steve Gergley's stories are meticulously weird, tender, and hilarious. Be careful with *The Great Atlantic Highway & Other Stories*—it will induce you down a stretch of interstate with exits that only lead to something strange and beautiful and exciting!"

—Shane Kowalski, author of *Small Moods*

"These stories are a little like if Tim Robinson went to get an MFA but was mostly too weird for the program and then wrote a book where he really got to let his voice shine instead of spending a couple years on SNL before *I Think You Should Leave*. Which is unfair and not-quite-right in a myriad of ways (to MFAs and SNL and Tim Robinson and Gergley himself and maybe even you?), but there's something about these stories that is both recognizable and not, both in the lineage of other favorites and also uniquely their own. These characters want to be human, but struggle at just how to do so, and their actions and decisions and the very mechanics of the story that are the most surreal are often the most honest and true, and also vice versa."

—Aaron Burch, author of *Year of the Buffalo*; editor of *HAD*

The Great Atlantic
Highway

AND OTHER STORIES

STEVE GERGLEY

Huge thanks to the editors of the journals in which these stories first appeared: "President Whitmore's Basement" in *Ligeia Magazine*; "Wes" in *HAD*; "A Face to Put on Top of Your Face" in *Storgy*; "On Location" in *Litro Magazine*; "I Smell Death on You" in *Bridge Eight Literary Magazine*; "Birthduty," "Canvas," and "The Blue Light" in *A-Minor Magazine*; "Apples," "The Great Atlantic Highway," and, "A Run to Ganymede," in *Bullshit Lit*; "A Text from Gina" and "Onward, to the Earth's Core!" in *Pithead Chapel*; "Security Questions" in *Drunk Monkeys*; "Theft at the Hardcore Show" in *Silent Auctions*; "Hanging," "Burning," and "Otherworld" in *Muskeg*; "Thin Man," "Richie's Vacation," and "Howdy Stranger, This is Howser" in *Misery Tourism*; "God's Thumb" in *Halfway Down the Stairs*; "Ghost Baby" and "Stroll" in *Ghost Parachute*; "The Statue" and "Window Teeth" in *Rejection Letters*; "On the River" in *BOMBFIRE*; "The Girl Who Was a Doorway" in *Asymmetry*; "Lunch Break" and "All the Things You Do" in *Remington Review*; "Meeting the Husband" in *Riggwelter*; "A Text from Zoey" in *Fictive Dream*; "Notes from the War," "What Remained After the Explosion," and "The People in the Walls" in *New World Writing*; "Brother Timothy Goes to the Batting Cages" in *Sledgehammer Lit*; "VanLife" in *Heavy Feather Review*; "Do You Like Death Metal?" "Thank You, Madame Clara," and, "Friday Night at the Pine Valley Mall" in *Maudlin House*; "Cicadas" and "Statues" collected as "Statues" in *No Contact*; "Dinner Date" in *Ellipsis Zine*; "Mirrors and More Mirrors" in *Fugitives & Futurists*; and "Thanksgiving Eve" in *Nymphs Publications*.

Table of Contents

PRESIDENT WHITMORE'S BASEMENT

Like where are the kids man.

Please . . . take whatever you want, just don't point that thing at me.

Man like I'll point it wherever I want, just like tell me where the kids are.

But what kids? I don't understand.

Don't bullshit me man.

I, I'm not, I just don't . . . there aren't any children here, I'm alone. I'm just staying in this house while—

You were great in *Independence Day* by the way.

Oh, I . . . well, thank you, yes that was—

Like I was only one when all that stuff happened, but I rewatch the movie a couple of times a year. My favorite part is that speech you gave right before the human race attacked the alien ships and won back our freedom. That was some George Washington shit right there, man. Gives me goosebumps every time I watch it.

Well, thank you, I'm glad the film resonat—

Man like so how long did it take you to write all those words and stuff for that speech.

Well, I think you may be a little bit confused about that, because I didn't actually write anythi—

I'm just asking because like English was always my worst subject in school. Anytime I tried to write something really cool like that speech of yours, the words always came out all mixed up and stuff, you know?

Yes, I . . . I think I know what you mean.

Like it always felt like no matter what I did, I could never find a way to get the words in my head out onto the paper in the right order.

Well, you're not alone. I know exactly how you feel. School can be tough for anyone.

But that's like why you're such a big hero of mine. You were able to inspire the whole human race to rise up and fight back against the aliens, and you did that with nothing but words.

Thank you, I'm . . . I'm just glad I could be an inspiration to—

Man like that's badass as hell.

I suppose that's one way to say it, yes. Thank you.

Like if I'm being honest man, I kind of feel like I failed our country by not being able to help out back then. I think I would've done good against those alien pricks.

Yes, well . . . I agree. You seem to be a very courageous young—

It's like an honor to be here man.

Thank you.

You were the best president until forty-five if you ask me.

Again, I'm very grateful, but you know it was just a—

Now like tell me where the kids are.

But that's what I've been trying to tell you, there aren't—

Don't bullshit me man.

I'm not, I just don't know what you're—

Are they in the attic or the basement?

But there aren't any—

Or is it some other secret room in here where you hide them.

There aren't any children in this house at all, it's not even my house. I'm just staying here for a few weeks while I work on this new project for—

Don't bullshit me man. I just watched *Independence Day* again last night, and you look exactly the same right now as you did thirty years ago. Like there's no way that's possible without the blood. Just ask a scientist.

With the ... what?

The blood, man.

What blood?

Don't bullshit me man.

I'm not, I—I honestly have no idea what you're talking about.

Like I don't have time to play your fucking mind games man, just tell me where the kids are!

Okay, okay, I think we got our wires crossed somehow, so why don't you just sit down, take a deep breath, and tell me exactly why you're here in my kitchen at ... three forty-six in the morning. Please. Help me understand.

Like don't even try to sweet talk me with your fancy words man! Like don't even try that garbage on me! You think that just because you were this great president who saved us from the aliens that that gives you the right to kidnap all these little kids and drink their blood for eternal life? That's not cool, man! Like you were my fucking hero growing up! How could you do this to me!

But that's ridiculous, you can't possibly believe something like—

Man like I told you to cut the shit with all your sweet talking fancy words!

Okay, I'm sorry, just please be careful with where you point that.

Like don't tell me what to do! I'll point it wherever I want! It's not 1996 anymore, you don't own me.

You're right, I'm sorry.

Whatever man, Christ. Now stand up and show me where the kids are.

But I . . .

Let's go. Chop chop.

Okay, I . . . I guess we can check the basement first.

Fine, whatever man, just like, you go first.

Okay . . . just be careful on your way down the staircase here. This is a very old house and some of the stairs look like they're uneven near the—

Oh God! Get the—get off, get off!

What happ—oh!

Oh my God!

Whoa, be careful, don't—

Goddamnit! Like move, move! Don't just stand there man!

Wait, I—what are you doing! Stop pushing so much!

Oh wow. I think it's dead.

What happened?

I think we're finally safe man.

What happened?

Like this huge spider landed right on my shoulder man.

God almighty. You nearly gave me a heart attack.

Like I know man, I hate those things. They give you diabetes if they bite you.

What? No they don't.

Yeah they do man, just ask a scientist. There's over a hundred million people in this country walking around with diabetes right now and they don't even know it. You think that's just like some super huge coincidence that happens by itself? Think about it. What's the one thing you can find inside every single house in America no matter where you live? The one thing that's in every house, apartment, Winnebago, and trailer home all across America? SPIDERS. Man like do you get it now? It's just basic science. There's no other way a hundred million people all spread out across the country could keep getting sick with this same unknown disease.

But it's not unknown at all. Type 2 diabetes, which is the type I assume you're talking about, is well understood by the medical community, and spiders have nothing to do with it. It's caused by obesity, poor diet, stress, genetics, lack of exercise, and—

Like that's bullshit man, you got to take off the blindfold the mainstream media has tied around your head. All that garbage you just said, that's a disinformation operation carried out by the deep state to keep us fat and lazy in our living rooms instead of out in the streets fighting back against their oppression. You should know this stuff better than anyone, you owned the government back in the day. Man like what's that.

This? It looks like a cabinet for storing dry goods, but like I told you, this isn't my house, so I'm not even supposed to be—

Is that where the kids are?

I can promise you that there are no—

Like don't bullshit me man!

I'm not bull—

Open it!

Okay, just—

Open it right now man, or it's your ass!

Okay. See? Just some soup mix and canned beans and dry spaghetti. No kids or blood or anything like that.

Whatever man. What's that over there.

That door?

Yeah. Where does that go.

I don't . . . why don't we find out?

Don't try to play those mind games with me again man.

I'm not, I just . . . can I ask you a question?

I don't know, can you?

I—

Yeah, not so smart now, are you, Mr. President? I can play mind games too.

What's your name?

What do you care?

Well, I just . . . since we've been talking for a while now and getting to know each other better, I just realized how rude I've been by never asking for your name.

Like whatever man, nobody cares. Now open that door and turn on the light.

Okay, but why do you think nobody cares about what your name is? I care.

Man like just . . . whatever. Nothing in my life matters anymore, so what difference does it make? This is the only thing I can do that actually means anything, because at least these kids are still young enough to have a—what's that.

It looks like a freezer. But why do you think that nothing in your life matters anymore? You're obviously a very courageous young man, and you seem to have a strong moral compass that—

Because like nothing does matter anymore man! This is all I have! Without this I just have a shitty job at Wal-Mart and a room in my parents' attic with my PC! All my friends are gone and married with kids and houses of their own, and I haven't even been on a date in twelve years! Like do you know what that feels like man? For women to be so disgusted by the sight of you that they turn their carts around in the supermarket just so they don't have to walk past you? Can you even imagine what it's like to be so alone for so long that you feel like you've been dead for a hundred years?

No, I . . . I'm so sorry you feel that way, I know how painful—

Like whatever man, I don't want to talk about it! Now open that freezer.

Okay, okay, just please be careful with where you point that.

Man like what the hell are these things!

I don't—it looks like meat, frozen—this must be their meat freezer, the owners of the house, I guess they like to hunt—

This is them, isn't it! Like this is what's left of all those kids you kidnapped, isn't it!

No, no, I swear on my life, this isn't even my house, I've never been down here, it's—

Like how could you do this to me! You were my hero, man! I loved you more than my own dad!

Look, please, just listen to me, it's not—it's venison, its deer meat, look! It says it right here on the plastic, it's deer meat from November of 2020, it's not—augggg!

Oh God.

Oh . . . oh . . .

Oh God man. Oh Jesus.

Please . . .

Like I'm sorry man, but you did this to yourself.

I . . . oh . . . please, please call . . .

Man like I'm sorry, but there's nothing I can do.

Please don't go . . . don't leave me like this.

I have to. It's for the kids. Saving them is the only thing I have left.

No, please . . . don't leave me alone down here.

Goodbye Mr. President.

WES

Just after college I got a job in a warehouse. I call it a warehouse but it was really just a barn on a rich old man's property. The old man and his son ran a business on the second floor of the barn, shipping makeup supplies all over the country.

Besides the old man and his son, there was only one other guy working there with me. His name was Wes. He was twenty-two, and he'd worked there for over five years.

Halfway through my first day of work, Wes led me into a tiny storage room and closed the door. Crouching down in the corner of the room, he reached into a cardboard box and handed me a brand-new box cutter sealed in crinkling plastic.

"Happy birthday, Sean," he said, grinning at me.

It wasn't my birthday, but I knew what he meant.

⌒──⌒

Two weeks later, on a slow February morning, Wes reached into his pocket and showed me something that looked like a small sheet of thick, white paper. From what

I could see, the paper was divided into a grid of one-inch blocks, like a book of stamps from the post office.

Wes grinned and asked me if I wanted some.

"What is it?" I said.

Wes grinned again, and then stepped up beside me and put his lips to my ear.

"It's acid," he said. "You want some?"

"Like LSD you mean?"

He nodded and grinned again.

"You want some?" he said.

"I don't think that's a good idea," I said. "We're on the clock until five."

He looked at me for a long while and then shook his head.

"God, you're boring," he said, slipping the paper back into his pocket. "No wonder the old man likes you so much."

He walked to the window and looked out over the snow-smothered lawn. A minute later he turned back to me and glanced down at his pocket. "Do you dare me to eat the whole thing?"

"No," I said. "That would be incredibly stupid, even for you."

"Will you give me a hundred dollars if I eat the whole thing?"

"I won't give you shit, so don't do it."

He looked down at his boots.

"How bout ten? Will you give me ten if I do it?"

"I'm not going to give you anything, Wes. And if you do take it, I'm going to tell the old man exactly what you did. So don't even think about it, dumbass."

He stared at me for a long time and nodded.

"You're a good friend, Sean. I hope you'll keep working here for a while. No one they hire ever lasts very long."

A few minutes later Wes went to the bathroom in the old man's house across the lawn. That was the only bathroom on site, and we were only allowed to use it a few times a day, so the bosses never said anything if one of us disappeared for a while to take a shit.

An hour later Wes finally came back to the barn. His face was as red as a baboon's ass, and his entire head was drenched in sweat.

"You fucking idiot," I said. "How much of it did you take?"

He smiled a huge, strange, intoxicated smile and reached into his pocket and showed me his empty hand.

"You fucking idiot," I said.

I looked around to make sure the old man and his son weren't watching us. Once I saw that they were busy in their offices, phones pressed to ears, I sat Wes down at the computer.

"Just sit here and pretend you're working," I said, placing his dripping hand on the mouse. "I'll take care of any orders that come in."

He looked up at me like an infant. His eyes were black. The pupils were so huge there was almost no white space remaining in either eye.

Seconds later he flew out of his chair, did fifty pushups in a minute, and flopped down in his chair again. Sweat scudded down his steaming face.

"You're a good friend, Sean," he said, breathing hard. "I love you so much. Am I going to die?"

"Okay buddy," I said, unsure of what else to say. "Just take it easy."

"I'm really scared, Sean, I think I'm going to die. I know I'm a piece of shit, but I don't want to die."

A new order came in. I grabbed the order sheet off the printer and looked around. The bosses were still in their offices, working.

"You're not going to die. Just put your sunglasses on and keep your mouth shut until it's over," I said. Then I grabbed three bottles of water from the open case under the desk and pressed one into his hands. "And you need to drink these waters. You should try to finish these three at least."

He took the bottle and guzzled the whole thing in one go. Then he grabbed my hand and squeezed hard.

"It's not just the acid Sean, I swear. I really do love you," he said. "You're my best friend in the world."

"Okay buddy," I said, patting him on the shoulder. "Just relax."

⌒～ ～⌒

A few hours later Wes finally came out of it. That evening we walked out to our cars together just like any other day, but this time we didn't talk much. I didn't really know what to say.

I quit the job a week later. I texted the old man's son and told him I'd found a better job somewhere else, but that was a lie. For the rest of that day I thought about calling up Wes to say goodbye, but I couldn't find the right words, so I never did. I haven't talked to him since.

A FACE TO PUT ON TOP OF YOUR FACE

When you were twelve you made a new face to put on top of your face. As far as you could tell there was nothing wrong with your face, it looked completely normal, just like everyone else's, but for some reason, nearly every time other people looked at you, they got angry. This had been happening for as long as you could remember, but lately things had been getting worse.

The first recent incident took place at your grandpa's funeral two months ago, when you couldn't stop grinning because that hilarious joke from *Spongebob* kept popping into your head. During the drive home, as your parents screamed at you about the immature, disrespectful faces you had made during the funeral, you cried and tried to tell them that you had been grinning not at Grandpa, but at the picture in your head of Squidward wearing a salmon suit. But they didn't listen. They just kept yelling.

The next incident happened a week later, when your dad took you to see that awesome new mummy movie with Brendan Frasier. This time you kept a straight face for the whole movie to make sure he wouldn't yell at you again. But somehow that was wrong too, and on the way home he yelled at you anyway, calling you a selfish little ingrate who doesn't appreciate anything.

So, since there seemed to be something seriously wrong with your face, you decided to make a new one.

That Christmas you asked your parents for an arts and crafts set. Following the big day, you spent the rest of your Christmas break in your room, building the new face. During those days you stood in front of your bedroom mirror for hours, testing out different smiles, different frowns, and different shapes of the eyebrows, all in the hope of finding a version of your face that no one could get angry at. By the time you went to bed each night, every part of your face ached from overuse.

On the morning of New Year's Eve you finally finished your new face. Sculpted from cheap clay, scaffolded with thin toothpicks, given depth and shape by rubber pencil erasers, and permanently frozen into an expression of safe neutrality, your new face wasn't a perfect disguise, but it would have to do. Your parents were taking you to your Uncle Ron's New Year's Eve party later tonight, and you didn't want to get yelled at again.

⌒⸺⸺⌒

To your surprise, the new face worked perfectly. No one seemed to know it was there. Moments after arriving at the party, your Uncle Ed pulled his nasty old trick of crushing your knuckles like grapes while shaking your hand, but since your new face hid your hot tears and the twisted scowl of pain flashing across your real face underneath, he quickly let go and tried the trick on another, more responsive kid.

Hours later, when your cousins Scott and Owen stole a bottle of vodka from the adult cooler and got caught drinking in the basement, the two boys tried to pin the crime on you. But thanks to your new face hiding the nervous sweat and frightened blush coloring your real face beneath, your Uncle Ron didn't believe them for a second, and he punished the true culprits instead.

After that day you wore your new face every time you left the house.

⌒— —⌒

Thanks to your new face, the rest of the school year went great. The kids in your class stopped making fun of you at school, and your teachers no longer got angry every time they looked in your direction.

Later that summer, after you'd had your friends over for a few sleepovers and a birthday pool party, you noticed that the new face worked on your parents too. So from then on you decided to wear the new face all the time.

After all, it felt nice to not get yelled at every day.

⌒— —⌒

Over the next few years, you kept working to improve your new face. As you spent more time among the normal, happy, non-threatening faces that constituted your high school social circle, these improvements became easier. So each night before bed, you stood in front of your bedroom mirror and carefully carved the day's improvements into your new face. Here you watched the excess clay curl from your fake cheeks in smooth, thin ribbons while your frozen expression gradually grew softer, more human, and more alive, than it had ever been before.

⌀——⌀

After college you got a job at the local CVS near your house. As a fine arts major with a focus in sculpture and pottery, you didn't yet have the money to open your own art studio, so you decided to live at home for a few years to save up as much money as you could.

But soon after you began work, customers started complaining about you. Each time there was a dispute over an incorrect price or an expired coupon, they would demand to speak to the manager. Once the manager arrived, the customer would yell about your careless attitude, your detached demeanor, and the way your dead-eyed expression made it seem like you weren't even listening to the words they were saying.

After two weeks of this, you considered telling your manager the whole embarrassing truth about your two faces. But there was a problem. Your new face had fused to your skin and could no longer be removed.

So, in order to save your job, you turned to the only thing you'd ever done right in your life: sculpture.

On your next day off from work, you drove around town and spent a few hours studying the behavior of the employees working in various retail stores. Standing in the quiet aisles, a small sketch pad clutched in your hand, you covertly drew reference figures of the employees' faces. Here you focused on the welcoming curl of the lips, the cheerful squint of the eyes, the thoughtful wrinkle of the brow.

Later, when you studied your drawings in the comfort and safety of your bedroom back home, you noticed that nearly every employee's face displayed the same fake, over-exaggerated expressions that only exist on television. Thinking about this, you remembered your old best friend Spongebob, and suddenly everything made a little more sense. Apparently a neutral face could only take you so far. If you wanted strangers to actually *like* you, you would need a face as expressive as a cartoon character.

For the rest of the night you closed yourself off in your basement workshop and built a third face to put on top of your other two. This time you used your reference figures to create a face as cheerful, expressive, and inviting as your favorite undersea sponge.

〇〜〜〇

For the next few years, your third face kept you out of trouble at work. Customers responded positively to your giant, permanent smile, and whenever a disagreement did crop up, you diffused it easily thanks to your perpetually cheerful expression that made each person feel like a respected and appreciated customer of the store. As a result of this improvement, you were promoted to assistant store manager at the beginning of your fourth year at CVS.

Despite this success at your day job, your dreams of opening your own art studio were no closer than they had been at the end of college. Even with the increased salary of an assistant store manager, you could barely keep up with your personal expenses and student loan payments.

On top of this, your personal life outside of work was nonexistent. You weren't exactly sure what the issue was in this department, but from past experience, you suspected it had something to do with your three faces. Whatever the problem, no one at work ever wanted to spend time with you after they clocked out. Each time you asked a coworker to hang out, they looked away from your grinning face and mumbled a vague excuse about being busy for the next few days.

So for the next five years you trudged through life without feeling much of anything. Each day was exactly the same as the one before it, and soon, the change of the seasons was the only way you felt the passage of time.

⌒— —⌒

Some time later, while taking the Grove Street curve on a snow-thickened morning in January, you lost control of your Toyota and barreled toward an eighty-foot oak standing on the side of the road. In a panic you stomped on the brake, but the pedal shuddered uselessly under your foot. The car continued its slide; the rear began to fishtail. You took a deep breath and looked out the window. The world lay choked with white, and the oncoming oak looked like the shaft of a brown arrow cutting sharply into the sky. Now you lifted your foot from the brake and finally admitted to yourself that you no longer cared whether you lived or died. Your life had become nothing more than an empty bag, a useless thing free of emotion and passion and love and meaning, and you couldn't think of a single reason to get all worked up about something so worthless.

An instant later you felt the impact. Metal crunched; glass shattered; icy air whirled around you; your seatbelt cut into your shoulder and drew blood.

For the next week you lay in a hospital bed and recovered. But every time your parents asked you to describe the accident, you stayed quiet. You didn't care about anything anymore, least of all yourself, so you didn't feel the need to explain anything. In the best case scenario, a full recovery would plant you right back in the same place you'd been for the past five years, completely alone in the world, working a job that meant nothing to you, so you kept your eyes closed and thought about nothing at all.

⌘

A week after leaving the hospital, your parents took you to see a therapist named Anna. You had not said a word in the two weeks since the accident, and your parents were worried about you.

You met with Anna on the third floor of a townhouse near the center of the Topine business district. She had straight blonde hair and looked to be ten or twelve years older than you. She was pretty and looked a little bit like an actress that had been in a comedy with Ben Stiller a few years ago, a movie you had seen in the theaters by yourself.

Since you no longer cared about anything anymore, you decided to answer Anna's questions. What did you have to lose? You told her about your car accident in the snow, and the moment during the skid when you stopped caring about your life. You told her about your worthless job at CVS, your nonexistent social life, your rotted aspirations of one day opening an art studio.

For the first few sessions you didn't see the point in any of this meandering conversation. But after a while it started to feel good to talk to a kind person who never felt the need to yell at you all the time.

At the beginning of your eighth session, Anna asked about your childhood. For a few minutes you omitted any mention of your replacement faces and instead talked about safe, inconsequential fluff, but soon you admitted the truth. It was the first time in your life you'd ever told anyone about your three faces.

"That's interesting," Anna said, after listening to the history of your faces. "Do you still use your alternate faces these days?"

You nodded.

"I wear the second one all the time," you said. "You're looking at it right now. But the third one is just for work."

"Wow, that's very impressive. You're a very talented artist."

"Thank you," you said.

Anna paused and looked down at her lap.

"I'm not sure if this will interest you or not," Anna said, looking up at you, her icy blue eyes shining, "but did you know that you're not the only person who does this?"

"What?"

"Well, I've never seen anyone take things quite as far as you did, but this is a common practice among individuals on the autism spectrum."

"What are you talking about?" you said, your heart smashing in your ears.

"I'm sorry, but we're at time. We'll have to pick this up next week. But let me write this down in case you want to read up on this stuff in the meantime," Anna said, leaning over her desk and scribbling some words on a purple post-it note. Then she swiveled around in her chair and handed the note to you.

You took the paper and looked down at it. Written in Anna's looping cursive were three words:

Autism Spectrum
Masking

But before you could say anything more, Anna opened the door and ushered you into the hallway.

❧

"So did you get a chance to take a look at those things I wrote down for you last time?" Anna said, moments after you sat down at the start of the following week's session.

"I did," you said, your heels bouncing nervously on the beige carpet. "It was pretty scary how accurate it was, you know, describing me and how I am."

"Good, I'm glad. And how do you feel, now that you know a little bit more about this stuff?"

You sighed.

"I feel angry and stupid and a lot of other things that aren't great, but there is something I want to try that might help alleviate some of these bad feelings," you said.

"Okay, sure. What do you want to do?"

"Well, this is probably going to sound pathetic, but over the last two months you've become the only person in my life I can actually call a friend, so I want you to be the first person in the past fifteen years to see my real face. Because if what you say is true, then that would mean there was nothing wrong with my face to begin with, and . . . I don't know. I guess I just want someone nice to see the real me for once."

Anna smiled at you and nodded.

"Absolutely. I'd very much like to see your real face."

"Okay," you said, blowing out a quivering breath. "The second face has been stuck to my real one for a long time, so this might take a while."

Anna leaned back in her chair and gave you a wincing smile.

"Okay, but be careful. Don't hurt yourself."

"Okay."

You took a deep breath and pressed your fingers into the smooth clay just in front of your ears. You couldn't remember how thick your second face was, so you pushed through the clay until you felt bone. Once there, you curled your fingers into a bowl and began to pull. Soon you heard the brittle crunch of toothpicks snapping, the suction-cup slurp of dry clay peeling from your skin. A crackling burn engulfed your head. Tears of pain collected in the corners of your eyes. Gritting your teeth against the searing pain, you suddenly grew impatient and claustrophobic; you couldn't bear to wear this awful thing for another moment. So you began tearing your second face away in chunks, your hands clawing at your cheeks. Once finished, the last bits of your second face lay piled in your lap, scattered on the carpet, and jammed beneath your fingernails.

It took a while for the pain to subside. Once it finally did, you opened your eyes and looked at Anna. But instead of her pretty face you saw the reflection of your own. She was holding a mirror in front of you.

Your real face looked horrible. The skin and muscle had rotted away, and all that was left was bloodblacked bone. Looking at yourself, you couldn't believe what you had become.

"How do you feel?" Anna asked from behind the mirror, her face still blocked by the horrifying image of your own.

"Oh my god," you said, as tears trickled down your destroyed face. "This is the most terrible thing I've ever seen."

"I didn't ask how you think you *look*," Anna said, her voice suddenly firm and forceful, more serious than you'd ever heard it. "I asked how you *feel*, now that you're not wearing a mask anymore."

For the next three minutes you stayed silent and thought about her question. Then, finally, you spoke.

"I'm afraid. I'm afraid of what people will say and how they'll treat me. But underneath that, I do feel a little better. I almost feel like an actual person again. And this is the first time I've felt like that in a very long time."

ON LOCATION

A month after I divorced my fourth husband, I earned the lead role in a gender-swapped remake of a wilderness survival film from the late nineties. For forty-five days we shot on location in Alaska, alongside a fifteen-hundred-pound Kodiak bear. It was a miserable shoot. We spent the majority of each endless day tramping through dense forests of spruce and pine, shambling over frozen outcroppings of sharp rocks, and plunging into arctic water so cold it numbed the skin on contact.

Copying Oliver Stone's method from *Platoon*, our director deepened the emotional desolation of our performances by shooting the film in the sequential order of the story, and then sending each actor back to L.A. immediately after their character died on camera.

By the beginning of the fourth week of the shoot, me and Larry II were the only two actors remaining on set. Because of my divorce, Larry's overprotective handlers, and the grueling difficulty of the first half of the shoot, I hadn't paid Larry much mind up until then. But once me and Larry started filming our scenes together, I was mesmerized by his graceful control of his body, his mastery of the craft of acting, and the breathtaking emotional nuance of his performance.

Since our characters were on opposite sides of the "survival equation," as the director described it, he didn't allow me and Larry to fraternize off camera. But I couldn't help myself. Something raw and hungry and primal had awakened inside me, and only Larry could satiate my need.

Later that week, as the midnight sun hung low and dim in the pale pink sky, I snuck in through the window of Larry's trailer. He was already awake. His big beautiful eyes stared at me the whole time, as if he knew I would come. I stared back at him. The woody musk of his body filled the chilly air. Stepping into a dull blade of light, I drew a deep breath and peeled the clothes from my body.

Larry's hot breath warmed my skin as he kissed my collarbone, my neck, the corners of my lips. Soon all the words I'd wanted to say for the past week came tumbling out of me. He took them in. Swallowed them as if they were nourishment. But he wanted more. So I gave him everything. I leaned my head back and offered myself to him. For a moment he paused, as if unsure of what to do. Then he eased me to the ground. He opened his massive mouth. He wrapped his jaws around my neck and gently started to squeeze.

I SMELL DEATH ON YOU

I was at my doctor's office for my yearly checkup. My doctor wore a salt-and-pepper beard, a stainless steel stethoscope, and a shimmering red tie that glinted like a stick of rock candy. His name was Tom Collins, like the drink. When Dr. Collins looked at my health report on the computer, his porcelain-white smile melted into a frown. He said my most recent labs showed a very high level of glucose in the blood. He said I was sixty pounds overweight. He said my body was already in a prediabetic state. Then he stared at me with a grave look on his handsome face and said I was on a bad path. As I looked down in shame at my aching, prediabetic toes that might not be here next year, I promised Dr. Collins I would start exercising tomorrow morning. I promised him things would be different around here. The here I was referring to was my body. To make this clear I gestured at my body when I said this. Neck to feet. *Here.* This was a stupid thing to say, but I savored the shame I felt from saying it. In my head I vowed to use that shame as fuel for me to change my ways. But then I remembered I had made this very same promise in this very same room at my last checkup a year ago. And that promise had obviously produced no results. That was okay though, because this time I meant it.

The next morning, I woke up before dawn and went for a walk. The only other person awake was a forty-year-old guy walking a white-and-gray Maine coon cat around the development. The guy had a pair of black-wired headphones jammed into his ears; his Maine coon wore a yellow harness connected to a dog leash. Just before we crossed paths, the guy stopped walking and let his cat sniff my ankles. I nodded at the guy and studied the yellow harness strapped around the cat's shoulders. After a while the cat looked up at me with his heterochromatic eyes (left eye: blue; right eye: green-gold) and said, in flawless English, "I smell death on you."

I looked up at the guy to see if he had heard what his cat had said to me. He hadn't. His headphones were connected to his phone, and he was staring at the screen and making sticky smacking sounds with his lips, as if he was very thirsty. When I caught a glimpse of his phone's screen, I saw writhing limbs and jerking bodies. It took me a few seconds to realize he was watching porn. I glanced down at his cat again.

"This is the only period of time he has to himself each day, what with work, and the wife and kids and such," the cat said, shaking his head and scratching his ear with his back claw. "So I let him do his thing. It's gross, I know, but we all have our needs."

"That makes sense," I said, nodding.

A short silence passed. I cleared my throat and looked up at the guy, but his gaze was still fixed on his phone. I turned my attention back to his cat.

"So about what you said before," I said.

"Yes that," the cat said. "You're wondering about life and death. About your legacy and purpose. About the dissipating scent of your ephemeral existence on this earth. You're curious about what it all means."

"I guess so. I'm just really worried because I had a check-up at my doctor's yesterday, and he said all these scary things about my health. He said I'm on a bad path. And then you, with what you said just now. It's a lot to take in," I said with a sigh. "And I know my life isn't anything special. I'll admit that in a second. I really just go to work, check on my fantasy baseball team, and see if any new players are available on the waiver-wire. Then I come home and stuff my face full of whatever's left in the fridge while I sit on the couch and click between the baseball games. On my TV I have the premium package of channels that lets me watch all the MLB games, even the ones on the west coast that start at ten. So I watch those and then I usually fall asleep around one or two and get up at seven and do the same thing the next day. If I'm being honest, my fantasy sports teams are the only things in my life that really matter anymore. But for some reason I'm still really scared of dying. I know this all sounds ridiculous. I'm sorry for babbling on for so long, but I have to know. Am I going to die soon?"

The cat licked his long, luxurious whiskers and yawned. He stretched his right paw forward and spread his bony cat fingers, showing me his hooked claws.

"We all die eventually," the cat said, walking to the strip of soft brown dirt at the edge of the lawn on my left. "Some of us sooner than others."

"That doesn't answer my question," I said, as fear and shame swirled in my head.

The cat scratched in the dirt for a while, squatted over the disturbed earth, and started to take a dump. The sharp, skunky smells of shit, cat urine, and scorched engine oil filled my nose. My face crunched into a grossed out scowl. The cat looked up at me and let out a shrill, angry meow.

"A little privacy?" he said.

⌒—⌒

A week later, I got a call from Dr. Collins's secretary. In a voice thick with emotion, she said that Dr. Collins had died of a ruptured brain aneurysm three days ago and that the practice was shutting down. The line went silent as she waited for me to say something, but I stayed quiet. I didn't want her to hear the relief in my voice.

The next morning I went for a walk before dawn again. I wanted to talk to the Maine coon about the Dr. Collins situation.

I circled the neighborhood four times, but I didn't see the porn guy or the Maine coon anywhere. An hour later, as I was pulling out of my driveway on the way to work, I saw the porn guy walking on the side of the street by himself. Pressing my foot to the brake, I lowered my window and waved him over.

"Hey man," I said. "Where's your cat? Is he too tired for a walk today?"

The guy looked up from his porn and stared at me with raw red eyes and a depressed frown.

"Roger slipped out the back door three days ago and a bear got him. It was fucking horrible. Me and Suzy and the kids have been bawling our eyes out ever since."

"Jesus," I said. "I'm so sorry. That's really fucked up. He was a cool cat."

The guy nodded, stared at the ground for a moment, and then turned back to his porn.

"Yeah," the guy said. "We didn't understand what he was talking about most of the time with all that philosophical stuff about life and death, but he was one of my best friends. It really hurts. I miss him."

"That sounds awful, I'm really sorry," I said, shifting my car into park. I squeezed the steering wheel as guilt and fear crashed over me. I didn't want to die. But at the same time, I didn't want Dr. Collins and Roger the cat to be dead instead of me, if it had been my time to go when Roger had sniffed my ankles last week.

I turned my attention back to the guy. Glancing in the side-view mirror, I saw that he had a full erection. Before I could avert my gaze, I caught him staring at me helplessly, like a lost child. Fat tears quivered in his eyes.

"I'm sorry," the guy said, shaking his head in shame. "My life is just so fucked right now. Work is a nightmare, and things are going to shit between me and the wife. Roger was the best thing in my life, and now he's gone."

"Don't worry about it, I understand," I said. Sick with guilt and pity, I leaned across the center column and clicked open the passenger door. "Do you want a ride back to your house?"

The guy looked at me and then down at the passenger seat and then back up at me. He drew a deep breath and shook his head.

"Thanks," he said, closing the door, "but no thanks. I've got to find a way to get through this on my own. That's the only way I'll make it."

"Okay," I said. I held his gaze for a long moment and nodded. "Good luck."

The guy gave me a weak smile and leaned his head through the open window of my car.

"Thanks," he said. "And by the way, you should probably get this thing checked out. Something in here smells like shit. Not like actual poop as in feces, but just bad. It's got a bad smell. You can smell it all the way out here in the street."

"Thanks for the heads-up," I said. "I'll look into it."

"Okay. See you around I guess," the guy said, knocking on the roof of my car. He folded his hands over his prominent erection and waddled away down the road.

Once the guy was gone, I shifted the car into drive, eased back into my driveway, and slipped the key from the ignition. Sniffing around the dashboard, I imagined Roger talking philosophy with Dr. Collins in heaven. I imagined Dr. Collins's perfect teeth shining like gemstones behind his lips. Then I imagined myself sitting next to them, checking my fantasy baseball team on my phone.

A faint smell of scorched engine oil seeped from the heating vent near the center column of the car. Not wanting to take any chances, I clicked off my seatbelt and decided to call out of work. This wouldn't be a problem.

Since I never went anywhere or did anything, I had plenty of vacation days saved up.

I slid my phone out of my pocket and called up my boss. My eyes slipped closed as I requested my day off. The smell of scorched engine oil grew stronger. On the phone, my boss's tiny voice complained about the lack of notice, but he agreed. When I opened my eyes moments later, I saw thick black smoke churning from the engine of my car.

BIRTHDUTY

When the blood stopped flowing from between my legs, the women of the plains burned down our hut and cast me naked into the woods. Since I had failed my birthduty by not producing a child in any of my forty seasons, I was no longer needed.

The next day my husband came to find me. Despite what the women had done to me, he still had permission to stay. *Men can father forever.* By his word this was what they had told him as their eyes glided over the sharp chevrons of his ribbed stomach, the ropy cords of his muscular builder's arms. To make him stay they offered him his choice of the younger women: women with full hips and taut breasts, women I had pulled from the womb twenty seasons ago, women who as girls had helped me shuck corn while asking about nothing but my lack of children. Over all this he chose me. Scared, angry, and relieved, I believed him. But as he held me close and guided me into the last of my scratchy clothes, I watched his eyes making measurements: he was scanning my saggy skin, cataloging every fold, calculating the costs and benefits of the decision he'd just made. Still, as we lay down together in the cool dirt later that night, he promised me he'd never leave.

༚— —༚

At daybreak I awoke. With heat on my skin I opened my eyes and watched the pink sun burn the charcoal-black from the sky. Pin oaks and sugar maples stood beside dogwoods and hackberries and sliced up the sheetlight flooding the woods. Dew-damp ferns dumped sparkling rainwater as I rolled onto my side and grasped for my husband beside me. Cold from the long night, my fingers craved the warmth of his work-rough palms, the springs of his curly hair; but the ground was empty, my hand clutching not his wrist but the warm dirt where he had lain. A part of me was surprised that he would do this, that he would go off and leave me alone, that the last words he spoke could have been anything but the truth. Thinking this, I heard his response in my head: *but it was true when I said it.*

Following the scent of his musk, I tracked my husband through the woods. As I walked, the sharp shells of acorns and hickory nuts cut into my bare feet. Wintergreen, wild sarsaparilla, may-apple, and corn mint lined the winding trail, but still I tasted him on my lips, smelled him in the crisp air. Soon I came to a clearing and the ground underfoot turned gray and flat and rock-like. Before me, standing in the center of this strange field, was a giant abandoned hut of wood and stone, a structure with a sloping triangular roof almost as tall as the trees. Wide square holes had been carved in rows of two and three into the front of this massive hut, and beneath these holes lay shards of dagger-sharp crystal. Being mindful of the sharp crystals, I crept up to one of the holes and peered through it. Inside was my husband, doing what he did best: taking stock, clearing rubbish, making order out of disorderly things. But he wasn't alone. With him was one of the young women from the plains, a headstrong girl named Sara, her hair thick and shining, as black as chipped obsidian, her body sleek and smooth, full with the vigor of young womanhood. Seeing her there I felt betrayed, enraged, but this time I was not surprised.

For hours I watched them clear the rubble from inside the massive hut. Together they heaved angled timbers, reams of insect-chewed cloth, and shafts of wood bent into the shape of a squatting man. They didn't speak a word to each other the entire time, but they didn't need to. Everything was said through the shimmer in their eyes, the frequent brush of fingers against skin.

As they worked, the air grew cold. Hard bulbs of gooseflesh sprouted on my skin, and thick snowflakes began to fall from the white sky.

Once they finished clearing the main area of the hut, they laid their clothes on the floor and made love. Watching them there I hoped I would finally discover what I had done wrong to fail in my birthduty of bringing a child into the world, but I learned nothing except how to hate the young for their youth. Minutes after they finished my husband sat up and looked right at me, but he made no acknowledgement of my presence. His eyes were blank, unseeing, as white as the falling snow.

Their child was born just before the pink sun vanished from the soap-white sky. It was a boy, his hair as black and thick as Sara's, curly like my husband's, his cry piercing and shrill and helpless, a sound urgent with want and hunger.

Outside, a foot of wet snow smothered the darkening world. With my feet and hands gone numb, I seemed to float just above the ground, a ghost not yet resigned to hell.

Back inside the hut, huddled with Sara near the far wall, my husband cradled his newborn son and slowly drifted to sleep. Seeing my chance, I moved. Minutes later my husband woke and peered around blindly for Sara. But he could not see that she was sprawled and unmoving on the floor, her slender body blacked with drying blood, her youthful skin painted gray and cold with death. From here I dragged her body into the snow, threw the bloodslick crystal into the woods, and took her place at my husband's side. Slowly, his heat laced life back into my limbs. Feeling my touch, he sighed in relief and contentment. I closed my eyes and rested. It would not be long until he discovered just how useful I could be.

APPLES

Me and Kyoko get into an argument about apples. She says Granny Smith are the best but she's wrong. To prove her wrongness I drive to Value King and buy a single Gala apple, a beautiful, firm globe of green-flecked red, and then I drive back home and bite into it. The crunch is exquisite and the flavor is a wonderful, complex tapestry of crispness, sweetness, and tartness mixed together in perfect proportion. I chew the large chunk of apple and swallow it and open my eyes and toss the apple to Kyoko, triumphant in my victory. The apple *thunks* against the living room floor and rolls under the rotting coffee table. Dust-drenched plastic clings to the musty furniture. The headlights of my car throw greasy brown light through the broken windows of the house.

THE GREAT ATLANTIC HIGHWAY

They built a two-lane highway across the Atlantic but the storms got really bad so they closed it down after a while. Me and Kyoko were driving from New York to London at the time, so we were the last car they let through in the eastbound lane. The drive was quiet and peaceful but the glare off the water was terrible and it was really hard to stay awake amid all that blue. Just before dawn on the second day of driving, a tropical storm came up from the gulf and flooded the gray string of highway before us. Kyoko stopped the car well short of the water, stared at the concrete median on our left, and sighed. The car rocked within the whirl of the powerful wind. Huge raindrops snapped like buckshot against the windows. Kyoko looked at me with a disbelieving smile and shifted into reverse.

A RUN TO GANYMEDE

On Saturday morning I go for a run out by the Miller Farm. Halfway through my run I run past a middle-aged guy running naked in the other direction. Though I avoid eye contact, the guy crosses the street and falls into stride beside me, his filthy Nike running shoes clomping loudly against the pavement. After a few seconds of silence, he says something I can't hear. I tug my left headphone out of my ear and ask him what he said. *Tomorrow is the day, Brother*, the naked guy says. Breathing hard, I squint at the guy through the blinding August sunlight. *What about tomorrow?* I say, not really wanting to know. *It's when Jesus will lead his flock back to his palace of gold on Ganymede. It's the glorious return to paradise, Brother*, the naked guy says, with a huge smile that droops like half-melted plastic. I give him a silent nod and stare down at the cracked pavement bouncing beneath my feet. When it becomes clear the guy won't go away until I say something more, I look up and ask, *What's Ganymede?* But instead of answering, the guy grins at me, points up at the sky, and suddenly veers off the road. Looking to my right, I watch the naked figure dash across the fallowing field, a cloud of brown dust swirling in his wake.

A TEXT FROM GINA

Just after one a.m. I'm in the basement smoking a bowl and playing Mario Kart with my buddy Denny when I get a text from this chick who says I got her pregnant. She tells me her name is Gina, but I don't know any Ginas. I pause the game and ask Denny if we know any Ginas. He tells me to stop bitching and to play the game and then he un-pauses without warning and Bowser rams me from behind and shoots me off the side of a cliff. As the fishing-pole cloud guy pulls me out of the abyss, I remember everything: Gina, her curly red hair, the bottle of warm triple sec, the accidental blast-off in the back seat of my car. My face goes hot and my hands start shaking. Staring at the TV, I see that in the span of about three seconds I've gone from first place with a big lead, to dead last with squid ink splattered across my half of the screen.

From very far away Denny says something and laughs, but I barely hear him. My mind is too busy screaming into the future at a million miles per hour, mourning my life and my dreams and all the things I'll never get to do if I have a kid. For a split second I see myself forty years from now, bald and fat and sixty-two, still driving a forklift over at the lumberyard. That sobers me up quick. Then, as the jazzy Mario Kart soundtrack plays on a loop in the background, the word pops into my head. In an instant I drop my controller and start typing a text to Gina:

I'm coming over. Where do you live

Before she can answer, I'm up the stairs, out the door, and running down the middle of the empty street, my footsteps clapping off the sloped pavement. With Denny's brother borrowing his car and mine in the shop, this is my only option.

The cool night air feels good on my face. It cuts past my cheeks smoothly, swiftly, hugging the contours of my head. Soon my eyes adjust to the oily scud of the night. In the black I see a boxy Subaru hatchback parked on the side of the street, a milk-white lion sculpture sitting atop a retaining wall. Looking at the row of lightless houses on the left, I imagine all the babies who could be inside those houses right now: babies wrapped in pink or blue blankets, babies wearing those dumb-looking winter caps, babies so fresh from the hospital that their wrinkled legs are still moist. Imagining all that, the word in my head takes on a whole new weight.

I take the right onto Darrin and head toward the exit of the development. Spotting a flickering light inside one of the houses, I stop running and look through the front window at the glowing rectangle of a TV. The image is blurred a bit by a pair of sheer curtains, but I can see the dashing characters, alien landscapes, and sparkling particle effects of someone playing a video game. Now my exhaustion catches up to me. In seconds my eyes slip closed and I rest my hands on my knees. Inside my head, I see myself playing Mario Kart with a tall, thin kid who I know is my future son. Here's me firing a shell and doing an obnoxious impression of Mario. There's him fighting a grin and telling me to shut up. Here's me jabbing his ribs and trying to pass on the right. There's him using a boost and winning the race by a nose.

I open my eyes and feel a hard, wet tightness rising in my throat. Suddenly sure of exactly what I want to do, I reach into my pocket and take out my phone. But before I can start typing a text to Gina, I see that there are six new messages from her waiting to be read:

Dont come over
My parents are really pissed and that would just make things worse
I'm getting it taken care of so you don't have to worry
Its expensive tho so I need you to pay half
I'll call you tomorrow Tom
Im sorry for texting so late I just thought you should know

I read her texts five times in a row to make sure I'm not hallucinating. After the fifth time through, the video game inside the house winks off with a splash of blue light. A few seconds after that, my heart slows for the first time since seeing Gina's original message. A wide grin slices across my face and I start laughing out loud. I can't help it. From here I try to text her back with a quick, *ok, talk to you tomorrow,* but for some reason the words blur and swim as I type them, so I decide to hold off and call Denny instead. He picks up on the third ring. When I start talking my voice comes out weird. It sounds hoarse and thick and honky, as if I'm sick and my nose is all stuffed up. Doing my best to sound normal, I tell him to start walking his ass toward Darrin Road. When he asks why I tell him to stop bitching and to bring his vaporizer.

SECURITY QUESTIONS

Security Question #1: who was the first boy/girl you ever kissed?

Answer: that's complicated

Sitting at the child-size desk her parents bought her back in sixth grade, her elderly laptop's dust-choked cooling fan filling the quiet room with a whisper of whirring sound, Adrienne closes her eyes and imagines she's locked in some kind of police station holding cell instead of her childhood bedroom in her parents' house back in her hometown of Topine, NY. And instead of the "Open New Checking Account" page of the Key Bank online banking website asking these questions in order to better protect her data, it's a gruff-looking TV detective in a beige trench coat who has the same voice as her ex-husband, Ray.

After quitting her job, torpedoing her marriage, and moving back home with her parents, these are the kinds of things Adrienne does now, to fill her empty days. Still, she can't deny that she needs her own bank account since she closed the joint one she had shared with Ray for the past two years. If she ever gets a new job, she's going to need somewhere for the direct deposit to go.

So, after she answers Detective Ray's first question with a non-committal *that's complicated*, he fires back with a series of quick, sharp questions in that too-high, embarrassingly emotional voice he used to slip into without realizing whenever they had a fight, the same voice that always made her picture him as a ten-year-old throwing a temper tantrum in the supermarket because his mom said no to that third box of Pop-Tarts.

Detective Ray: who was the first boy/girl you ever kissed?

(This is actually not too far off from reality; he really would ask a pointless question like this, as if it mattered somehow.)

Adrienne: that's complicated.

Detective Ray: (yelling in the screechy, too-emotional voice of a spoiled ten-year-old) *why?*

Detective Ray: why is it so complicated, Adrienne?

Detective Ray: it's a very simple question!

Detective Ray: why do you always have to make everything *so complicated?*

Since she has neither the strength nor the patience to deal with real life right now, Adrienne keeps going with this dumbass simulation.

(Do other people actually do this or is it just her?)

Adrienne: I'm not trying to make it, or anything else, more complicated than it needs to be. The problem is with the question, Ray. It's vague.

Detective Ray: how is the question vague?

Adrienne: it's vague because you're not specifying whether you're asking for the name of the first boy *I kissed, or the first* girl *I kissed, and that's relevant because the answer is different for each of those things.*

57

Detective Ray: Jesus Christ, how many people have you—

Detective Ray and the holding cell disappear and now she's just think-talking into the reddish-black void behind her closed eyelids.

Adrienne: if you're asking for the name of the first person I ever kissed, either boy or girl, then the answer to that would be Milly Campbell behind the big sugar maple in her back yard in fourth grade when we were asking each other which boy in our class we liked and then we both said Matty Pierce at the same time and giggled and I felt the warm burn of jealousy in my face and chest because Milly was the prettiest girl in class with her long, shiny, chestnut hair and her beautiful blue eyes that looked like gems. So to freak Milly out and to knock the little princess off her royal pedestal that all the boys (including Matty Pierce) had put her on, I suggested that we maybe try practicing kissing on each other in case either of us ever got the chance to kiss Matty in the future. Hearing that, Milly blushed and pursed her face up into a lemony scowl and said she wanted to save her first kiss for Matty, but that was the wrong thing to say because it just made me want to hurt her more for liking the same boy I did because I knew he would like her back instead of me, so I leaned forward and kind of mashed my lips against Milly's for a very long three seconds and then I pulled my face away from hers and looked up at the sun shining on the maple leaves swaying above our heads and I saw how the light made some of the leaves glow a translucent yellow-green and how the veins in the leaves branched out all straight and sharp just like the veins in my dad's hairy legs that I would always find myself staring at whenever he mowed the lawn. And then after a second I remembered about Milly and the kiss so I ran over to the swing set near the back deck and started swinging as hard as I could as if nothing weird had happened. So if that's *what you're asking, Ray, then Milly Campbell in fourth grade behind the sugar maple in her back yard would be my answer.*

Detective Ray: (he's back now so he can gape, speechless, at her badass answer she could never come up with in the moment when he would ask infuriating, pointless questions like this) *that's not really the question I was asking—*

He disappears again to let Adrienne speak.

Adrienne: okay, well, if that's *not what you're asking, then I guess my answer would be Matty Pierce in the middle school library two years later during study hall when he was looking for a book about his favorite animal, the arctic fox. That was my favorite animal for a while too, because it was his, and also because it was cute. And he was officially dating Milly at the time, so there's that, but I know for a fact that they hadn't kissed yet by the time I kissed him in the library (he told me it was his first kiss), so even though Milly got to be his girlfriend first, I actually—*

Adrienne feels herself smile at this thought.

Detective Ray: won?

Adrienne: no one ever said it was a contest.

Detective Ray: (now acting as more of a confidant/ therapist since her anger at him is gone for the moment) *but that's what you were thinking.*

Adrienne: so what. I told you it was complicated.

With these thoughts in mind, Adrienne opens her eyes, leans over her laptop, and types an answer to the first security question.

Security Question #1: who was the first boy/girl you ever kissed?

Answer: milly c

Now Adrienne turns her attention to the next security question.

Security Question #2: in what town/city did you first meet your spouse?

Answer: another tough one

Detective Ray: (suddenly back to his angry, judgmental self) *how is this one tough? I don't think it's that hard to remember where we met. Or have you just had so many spouses that it's hard to keep it all straight in your head? Christ Almighty, it must be nice to have fucked so many guys that you can't even remember where you met each akhsl fhsf ynai shlf kahsdfidf . . .* (this is her trying to make him disappear again, but for some reason he stubbornly stays where he is and keeps talking) *. . . was still a virgin in my second year of community college when I met you. You want to know how many girlfriends I'd had before then?*

He doesn't wait for her answer.

Detective Ray: two. Two girlfriends and all I ever got was a few toothy BJs because I was her first boyfriend and she didn't know what she was doing when it came to—

To shut him up Adrienne opens her eyes and takes the pillow from her bed and lays down on the floor of her room. Here she stretches her wiry runner's legs all the way to the wall and looking up at the window behind her sixth grade desk she winces in the hard glare of the noon sunlight cutting through the stacked slats there and moments after this she takes a long, slow, deep breath in and holds it for a count of one . . . two . . . three . . . four . . .

and lets it out slowly. Once this is done, Ray finally stops talking. So she closes her eyes again and continues with the simulation (which, if she's being honest [and why shouldn't she be? with her parents at work it's not like there's anyone else around to witness this] she's really starting to enjoy all this nonsense in that quintessential Adrienne way of savoring the pathetic/blackly comic absurdities of her own pain and weirdness).

So, continuing with the simulation, Adrienne turns her attention back to the original question Ray had asked her, the one about where she met her spouse. Thinking about it, she admits to herself that yes, for most people (including Ray) that should be an easy thing to answer, but for her it's not. How many other girls can say they're both twice-married and twice-divorced by the age of twenty-seven? Not many. But that's what Ray doesn't—

She feels herself smile again and in an instant she's back in the holding cell with Ray, but this time he's not wearing the TV detective trench coat (she really has to stop watching those stupid *Law and Order* crime shows with her parents every night) and he seems tamer and more caring, like the sweet version of him that she once convinced herself she loved.

Adrienne: it's a tough question for a few reasons, Ray. One, we're no longer married, so I don't think I can call you my spouse anymore (did she ever once think or say that word in reference to him over the entire two years they were married?) ...

She speaks the word out loud to test this theory and it feels as alien and strange as a dead salmon in her mouth. (That's a no.)

Adrienne: . . . and two, you're not the only man I've ever been married to.

Adrienne opens her eyes to skip all the angry blathering the real Ray would launch into at the utterance of this sentence, but instead her simulation of him stays sweet and he doesn't say a word and her mind is clear and quiet and the house around her is still. Outside, a bird trills brightly; she savors the natural, calming sound. Then she closes her eyes once again and tells the sweet version of Ray the story of her first marriage.

Adrienne: I never told you about this because I don't really understand why I did it myself. But when I was nineteen, I didn't know what I was doing with my life and I thought I'd made a big mistake by going to college for political science like my parents had wanted me to (they wanted me to be a lawyer), so I kind of freaked out and informally dropped out of school by moving in with this older guy who lived in my college town. This was before I moved back home and started up at Topine CC where I met you. But this guy was nice to me and I thought I could escape from real life by staying with him so one day I asked him to marry me and he said yes and we got married.

Sweet Ray: wow, I . . . that's pretty crazy Rin, I never knew that. But I'm really sorry it didn't work out. I can see how that would make this question more complicated.

Adrienne: the marriage only lasted nine days and he was very kind and understanding and he paid for everything concerning the divorce and then I dropped out of college for real and moved back home to Topine and we've never talked since then so it doesn't matter. His name was Gene by the way. Is. Is Gene. I don't think he's dead because he was only fifteen or twenty years older than me, but who knows. I hope not. He was a very nice person. So that's the story. I really don't try to make things complicated, they just kind of turn out that way with me. As you know.

The simulation of Sweet Ray smiles and nods slowly, knowingly, and thoughtfully, as if he understands everything and the next words he says will solve all her problems in an instant. Seeing this in her head, Adrienne feels herself smile. She suddenly remembers why she once loved this man and asked him to marry her. (Which is apparently a habit of hers.)

Sweet Ray: . . .

She waits a long time but she doesn't know what he would say in this situation, so she sits up, tosses the pillow back onto her bed, clambers into her chair, and stares at the two remaining security questions on the screen.

After a long minute, she scoffs to herself and shakes her head.

"Fuck it, maybe it's not that complicated after all."

Security Question #2: in what town/city did you first meet your spouse?

Answer: topine

Security Question #3: what was the name of the street you lived on in third grade?

Answer: cambrian heights

THEFT AT THE HARDCORE SHOW

Six months after her best friend Leanne killed herself in a Holiday Inn off Route 17 in New Jersey, Dawn played with her band in her first local hardcore show. It was a sweltering Friday night in June, and there were about eleven people standing in the dim backroom of The Luna Café, a small coffee shop stranded at the end of a strip mall on the southern edge of Dawn's hometown of Topine, NY.

From where Dawn stood in the back corner of the room (there was no stage; the band stood on the same weathered floorboards as the crowd), the entire place smelled like cigarettes and sweat and body odor. But she didn't care about that. All that mattered to her right now was the blast and crash of Luke's drums, the sludgy hum of Gabe's bass, the roar and squeal of her downtuned guitar, and the corrosive anger trapped in her chest. Because ever since Leanne had dipped her sliced wrist into a tub of warm bathwater during the early morning hours of January eighth, Dawn had been angry: angry at herself for not seeing the signs, angry at the world for being indifferent to Leanne's pain, angry at the heartless fucks who had bullied Leanne into taking her own life. And it was this anger that fueled Dawn's performance tonight.

Ten minutes into their set, as the band launched into the chugging intro of "Terminal Velocity," the best original they'd written in their four months together, Dawn saw a group of six or seven teenage boys crowding near the wall on the opposite side of the room. For the next few minutes these boys stared at her, talked among themselves, and grinned like fools. Near the end of the song, an older boy in the group gestured with his head toward the messy pile of the band's personal items that stood in the corner of the room. Seeing this, Dawn stopped playing the song, pulled Gabe's mic from its stand, and spoke directly to the boys who'd been watching her. From her years of experience dealing with asshole guys in high school, she already knew exactly what they were going to do next.

"Don't. Touch. Our goddamn. Shit," she said into the mic, slowly enunciating each syllable, her voice trembling with nerves and anger. Now she pointed at the group of boys. "Yeah. I'm talking to you. Don't do it. This is the only warning you're going to get."

Moments after she said this, the boys burst out laughing. Within their laughter one of them yelled a sarcastic, "Oh ho ho!", while another smacked his hand over his mouth in mock terror and swiveled his head left and right. Both of these reactions prompted more wild laughter from nearly every boy in the group, all except one. The only one who didn't laugh was a short, wiry, long-haired boy of about fourteen. A few strings of shiny black hair rested on the boy's shoulders, and a muddy smear of a mustache sprouted just above his upper lip. Seeing this boy, noticing the pained look of discomfort on his face, observing the way he crossed his arms and turned his body away from the rest of the group as if trying to disassociate himself from their obnoxious behavior, Dawn felt her anger dissipate a little bit. Forever an outsider herself, she knew exactly how it felt to be trapped in the black-haired boy's situation, constantly torn in opposite directions, loneliness and isolation on one side, the craving for social approval on the other, your morals, your beliefs, and the kind of person you want to be stuck in the middle. Looking at him there she hoped he would someday find a Leanne of his own, a friend who could help him survive all the upcoming nonsense of his high school years.

Dawn nodded at the black-haired boy.

"For everyone else, I just want to say thanks for coming out to our first show. We're Severe Tire Damage, and this next one is called, 'The Bone Dance.' Bonus points to anyone who gets the joke." She waited a beat to see if the boy would react in any way, but he didn't. Neither did anyone else. Assholes. No one but Leanne ever seemed to appreciate her sense of humor.

Dawn handed the mic back to Gabe and started playing the intro to "The Bone Dance." Out of the corner of her eye, she watched Gabe shake his head and mouth some words to Luke.

I'm so sick of her shit.

Upon seeing this, she turned and stared them both down, challenging them to talk their trash to her face, but as usual they pussed out. Why does every single person in her life have to be an asshole?

About a minute later, as Dawn clawed at her Ibanez and filled the room with granite-heavy slabs of palm-muted power chords, a few of the obnoxious boys started waving at her. One swung his arms over his head like a starving man stranded on a desert island; another made a V with his middle and index fingers and flicked his tongue through the middle. Thoroughly sick of these fools, Dawn shook her head in disgust and stared down at her fretboard. A few seconds later she noticed a dark flash of movement in her periphery. When she looked up, she saw the black-haired boy hunched over the pile of her band's things. Unlatching the silver clasps of Dawn's guitar case, the boy reached inside, and pulled out the hoodie she had put there just before the show. Now he bunched the hoodie into a ball and jammed it into his rank and sweaty armpit. Seconds later he was gone, dashing past the group of waving boys, darting between the scattered kids in the room, scampering into the lighted front of the café, and streaking by the baristas as they wiped down the counter with rags.

Watching this theft unfold in real time, Dawn didn't hesitate. In an instant she stopped playing the song, unplugged her guitar with a squeal of feedback, and threw it to the floor. Startled by the sudden screech of feedback, Gabe and Luke stopped playing a moment before Dawn's Ibanez hit the ground; in this quiet Dawn savored the sound of the impact. After hardcore music, smashing something valuable was the second-most effective way for Dawn to vent her anger these days; but at nineteen years old she didn't have much money and didn't own anything she could afford to lose, so she almost never had the chance to break anything. But this time was different. What had just happened to her was an outrage, an injustice, so her actions were not only justified, but necessary. So in the spirit of satisfaction, she stood there for an extra few seconds and listened to the crackling of the fracturing wood, the dissonant *sprung* of the breaking strings, and the flying apart of this two-thousand-dollar thing she'd spent six months saving up for.

Once this moment was over, she was off. Running heavy-footed and furious toward the front of the café, she shoved aside anyone who stood in her path. Seven seconds later, as she glided through the café's doorway and listened to the creaking wooden door swing closed behind her, she heard Gabe yell into his microphone.

What the fuck, Dawn!

⌒— —⌒

Out on the sidewalk, the June heat clung to Dawn's skin like a bedsheet dipped in maple syrup. Through the ringing in her ears Dawn heard the clapping echo of the black-haired boy's sneakers snapping against the concrete. Now she ran down the sidewalk after him, her legs aching sour and cold, her heart banging hard behind her ribs. Slippery sweat soaked into her shirt, her jeans, the spaces between her toes.

Dawn looked ahead to the far side of the strip mall. There she saw an idling car sitting in the parking lot near the end of the building. The car was a maroon Honda from the early 2000s, and a complete piece of shit: a set of three, neon-green bungee cords tied the warped rear fender to the maroon body; a fat scramble of clear packing tape sealed closed the passenger-side door; and the red-glass globes of both taillights had been punched out. In an instant Dawn knew this was the boy's destination—only high school boys drive a car like that—so she veered to the right and swung out into the parking lot, dashing straight for the idling car. If she could get there before he did, she'd be able to cut him off and get back her goddamn hoodie.

Moments later the boy looked to his right and saw Dawn clomping across the parking lot. Her face was tight with fury, and her cheeks were the same color as tomato soup. Seeing her there the boy scrabbled to a skidding stop, abruptly changed direction, and ducked into Geno's Third, a pizza parlor that was the last store still open in the strip mall.

Thirty seconds passed before Dawn pulled open the front door of Geno's Third. Hearing the sounds of yelling voices and clattering pans coming from the kitchen, she pressed a damp palm into the wall and swung behind the front counter. The heavy smells of tomato sauce, melting cheese, grilled meat, and raw dough enveloped her head as she trudged past a flour-dusted prep station. A wall of standing heat radiated from a brick oven on her right. Two teenage girls dressed all in black stared at her in silence and pointed at an open door at the back of the kitchen. She gulped a wheezing breath and nodded at them in thanks.

Dawn stepped through the back door of Geno's Third and out into the rear parking lot of the strip mall. A rusting green dumpster stood at the far end of the pavement, and an overhead sodium lamp bathed the entire lot in an orange glow. Standing a few feet to the left of the door was a tall man wearing a Geno's Third t-shirt, a pair of camo cargo shorts, and a backward baseball hat. Bunched in the man's fist was the collar of the black-haired boy's t-shirt. A burning cigarette dangled between the man's lips.

The black-haired boy saw Dawn first.

"Oh shit," he said, squirming in his stretched t-shirt, Dawn's hoodie still jammed under his arm.

Without loosening his grip on the black-haired boy's collar, the smoking man turned around.

"Are you the one who was chasing him?"

"Yeah," Dawn said, huffing a shallow breath. Her heart was still blasting away from the run, but at least she could talk now.

"What the hell did he do?"

"He stole my goddamn hoodie while I was playing in the show with my band," she said, stepping forward and wrenching her hoodie from under the boy's arm. She glanced up at him. A thin coating of sweat glazed his face, and his lips were curled into a cocky little smile. Looking into his eyes, she remembered the strange connection she'd felt with him before the theft, and suddenly she felt like the biggest fool in the world. So she punched him in the balls.

The black-haired boy coughed out a wet groan and crumpled to his knees.

"That's what you get for stealing my stuff, dickhead."

The smoking man let go of the boy's shirt and took a step back.

"Jesus," he said. He tossed his cigarette in the direction of the dumpster and backed toward the rear door of Geno's Third. "I'm going to let you two work this out between yourselves. But I don't want to be finding any dead bodies out here when I open up tomorrow morning, you got it?"

Dawn nodded at the man as he disappeared behind the closing door.

Satisfied that the black-haired boy had gotten what he deserved, Dawn turned around and started walking away. A few seconds later, he spoke.

"It was just a prank. You didn't have to go all Texas Chainsaw Massacre on me about it," he said with a cough, his voice reedy and defiant. "It's your own fault for even bringing a hoodie tonight, anyway. Who does that? It's like eight hundred degrees out here."

Dawn stopped walking and turned around. Though she knew it was a bad idea to even acknowledge him anymore, she couldn't help herself.

"Not that it's any of your business, but I bring this hoodie with me everywhere because it's the last thing my best friend gave me before she took her own life six months ago," Dawn said, pressing the balled sweatshirt to her chest. "So it's pretty goddamn important to me."

"Geez," the boy said. "Is that true?"

"Of course it's true, jackass. And the only reason she did that is because assholes like you thought it was funny to constantly talk shit about her. And now she's dead. So you should be thankful that all you got was a punch in the balls."

Dawn's eyes started to burn with collecting tears, so she turned around. She didn't want this scumbag thief to see her crying.

"If it makes you feel any better, it wasn't my idea," he said from behind. "Taking your sweatshirt I mean. My friends made me do it. And now that I think about it, you're right. They are assholes."

Dawn scoffed at this and shook her head.

"Unless they put a gun to your head, they didn't *make* you do anything. You did it yourself. So that makes you the biggest asshole out of all of them," she said without turning around.

A breeze kicked up. Dawn closed her eyes and drew in a deep breath as cool air cut past her glowing cheeks, her pounding temples.

"I guess, but couldn't I say the same thing about you? Didn't you screw over the guys in your band by stopping in the middle of a song to chase after me?"

Dawn opened her eyes and turned around. The black-haired boy was now on his hands and knees near the dumpster, holding the half-smoked cigarette the smoking man had flicked away a minute ago.

"That's completely different. I'm the victim in this case. You stole something very valuable to me, and I was just trying to get it back. I didn't do anything wrong," Dawn said, her anger quickly rising again.

The black-haired boy stood up and slapped his knees clean with his free hand. Then he cocked his head to the side and pointed at Dawn with the half-smoked cigarette clamped between his index and middle fingers.

"Exactly. In *your* mind you didn't do anything wrong. But what about in the minds of your bandmates? I don't know about you, but I haven't heard any music playing since we've been out here, so I'd guess they're pretty pissed at you right now for screwing up their show," he said.

He raised the half-smoked cigarette to his nose and sniffed at it.

"Do you have a light?"

Dawn shook her head in disgust and rubbed her aching eyes.

"I can't believe I wasted a single moment of my life listening to this shit."

She turned around and started walking away again.

"Don't worry, you're not alone," the black-haired boy said to her back. "Nobody ever thinks *they're* the asshole. It's always someone else, right?"

⌒⸺⌒

Dawn walked up to the front door of The Luna Café fifteen minutes later. Her legs were stiff and screaming from the run, and she could already tell she'd have trouble walking tomorrow. The two baristas she'd run past earlier leaned against the wall next to the door, smoking.

"No one in your band is allowed to leave until you clean up your mess in there, so you need to get on that shit ASAP," the older barista said to her.

Inside, the café was empty. Upside-down chairs stood on every table except one. Gabe and Luke sat across from each other at the last table, staring at their phones.

"We can't leave until you clean up your mess over there," Gabe said.

"I know. They told me."

"Well, do it fast. I've got to open the store at seven, so I'd like to get five fucking hours of sleep tonight."

"Alright, chill out. I'm on it," Dawn said.

"And just so you know, we put out an ad on Twitter for a new guitarist. For obvious reasons."

Dawn grabbed her guitar case from the corner of the back room.

"Has anyone answered?"

"We just tweeted it like thirteen minutes ago. But no. No one has answered yet."

Dawn kneeled in front of her broken Ibanez and opened her hardshell case. She draped her hoodie inside the case and smoothed the wrinkles from the black fabric. It was calming and therapeutic to do this, to feel the damp cloth gliding beneath her calloused fingers, and for the first time in months, she didn't feel angry anymore.

Now she drew a slow breath and examined her broken guitar.

The angled headstock had snapped off just above the nut, and a six-inch crack sliced down the back of the neck. Other than that, the body seemed to be okay. With a new neck and the right parts, maybe it could even be fixed.

Thinking this, Dawn remembered the black-haired boy's words. Moments later, she spoke.

"If I said I'm sorry, would you guys give me another chance?"

HANGING

I am the hanging man. For two days I've hung from this elm. There's a rope around my ruined neck. Flies walk on my open eyes.

I am the first one you see from the road. He put me here to let you know: the angel of God has come to this place. To revel in sin is to end up like me.

I've lived in this town my whole life. Just before I turned sixteen, I met God in a dream. His body was wrapped in shining gold. His face was the face of the father I'd never known.

The next day I walked to the wooden church at the top of the hill. It was Sunday, and the entire town was gathered for mass.

Near the end of the preacher's sermon my body began to shake. Moments later I found myself at the front of the church, speaking God's words. To this day I don't remember what He said. All I remember is the feeling of His voice passing through me, His words flowing from my mouth like cold water in a creek.

For the next twenty years, I stood before my neighbors and preached my Father's good word.

On the morning of my thirty-sixth birthday, His voice suddenly left me. So I tramped through the woods until I found a creek. There I stepped into the clear water, rested my head on the rocks, and began to pray.

For two days I lay in that creek and let my Father's water wash over me, just as his spirit had washed over me on that day twenty years ago. Shivering in the icy water, I heard nothing but the bubbling mumble of the creek, the rasping breath of the wind. But still I stayed, staring up through the trees.

On the morning of the third day a column of fire came down from the sky. Upon seeing this, I ran back to town and gathered my congregation at my church. Minutes later an angel of God arrived at our door. His body was wrapped in gold; His face glowed with God's light. In an instant I recognized Him: He was my Father, the one who had appeared in my dream all those years ago.

Overcome with joy, I opened my arms and let Him inside.

BURNING

I am the burning man. For hours I've sat on this slab of scorched earth that used to be our church. Here I stare at His brilliant light, His glittering gold, His beautiful face.

His face is the face of man, woman, and child united as one spirit under God. He is God's angel sent down from the sky.

My legs are afire. My fingers are swallowed in flame. But still I stare at Him. His beautiful face fills my heart with light and love and peace and divinity. When I try to turn away, the world begins to bend.

Just before sunset he looks down at me. Staring into His golden eyes, I hear His voice in my head. His voice is the voice of God. With this voice He tells me to stand up and to fetch a rope and to hang the false prophet from a tree.

I try to follow His command, but my body doesn't move. It roars with pain. It shrivels and shudders within the crackle of the divine flames. Seeing this, God's angel walks up to me and touches my shoulder. His touch is cool, soothing, the touch of a loving father comforting his frightened child. In an instant the pain of my burning body washes away and I can move again. Rapturous with joy, I follow my Father's command. I walk to my house on trembling, burning legs and grab a length of rope from my barn. Clutching the rope in my blackened fingers, I stare in awe at the power of God's will: the rope does not burn.

Now I return to our destroyed church and wrap the rope around the false prophet's neck. I drag him to the edge of town and hang him from a sturdy elm. Once I am finished, God's angel appears before me and rests His hand on my head. A deafening peal of thunder cleaves the world in two. A wall of gold light swallows my body whole. I fall into God's arms and everything disappears.

DO YOU LIKE DEATH METAL?

A few weeks after me and Kyoko got back together for the second time, we went to the wedding for one of her friends from work, a twenty-nine year-old forensic pathologist named Jenny. Kyoko hadn't put her wedding ring back on yet, and we still hadn't sorted out any of our old communication problems, so I kept my guard up. After everything that had happened between us over the past ten years, I was afraid of letting her back in too quick.

Seated beside us at the reception was my sister's best friend from middle school and a tall, skinny guy who said he was her husband. Once me and my sister's friend had exhausted all the pleasantries and stilted small talk demanded by the occasion, the husband turned to me and grinned.

"Do you like death metal?" he said, leaning back in his chair and shredding on an invisible guitar.

Our table sat at the edge of the dance floor. Thumping electronic dance music roared in my ears, so I had to read his lips to understand what he was saying.

"Not really, I listen to jazz mostly," I shouted. "I used to play piano in a jazz trio a bunch of years ago, but I had to give it up to—"

"Yo, you got to listen to this, then," he said, handing me a tiny red thing that looked like a plastic kidney bean. He pointed at the kidney bean thing and then to my right ear. "Try it. Since you're a musician, I'm pretty sure you're the one person here who'll actually appreciate it."

I stuck the kidney bean thing in my ear.

Moments later the husband's body dissolved into a cloud of gold dust. Kyoko and my sister's friend were looking at pictures on Kyoko's phone, so they went on talking as if nothing had happened. Sinking to the ground, the cloud of glittering dust hovered across the crowded dance floor and seeped through the grille of one of the thumping speakers. Soon the pulsing dance music morphed into a dizzying cacophony of alien screams, razor-wire guitar, polyrhythmic drum grooves, and atonal piano arpeggios.

When I pressed my hands to my ears in surprise, Kyoko turned to me with a look of concern.

You okay? she mouthed.

I pointed to the speakers behind us.

What? she said, with a shrug and a shake of her head.

"Can't you hear the—" I shouted, but then the alien music was abruptly cut off by the intro to Lady Gaga's "Bad Romance."

Kyoko squealed with delight and grabbed my hand.

"Holy shit, I love this song! We have to dance to this right now!" Kyoko yelled at me, her eyes glazed and glowing, her cheeks as red as the dregs of wine sitting in her empty glass before her.

When I turned back to the chair beside me, the husband was sitting there once again, back in human

80

form, gesturing with his head at the speakers from which his alien death metal had been blaring moments ago.

"So, how'd you like it?"

"I wasn't a huge fan of the vocals, but it was pretty interesting, musically. I really liked the piano parts."

"Hell yeah, man," he said, "there's a lot of good shit out there in the universe."

"Yeah," I said, glancing over at Kyoko, who writhed in her chair to the rhythm of Lady Gaga's music. "Do you want your headphone back?"

Keep it, the husband mouthed, with a grin. Then he took a drink of water from his glass and turned back to his wife. Before I could ask him any of the thousand questions flying through my head, Kyoko popped out of her chair and started tugging me onto the dance floor.

"Come on, Nick! We're missing the whole song!" she said, happily drunk, her warm hand wrapped tightly around mine.

THIN MAN

On the way home from her morning shift at Value King, Kyoko bought me a copy of the *Topine Transcontinental Tribune*, our local tabloid newspaper.

I'd been reading the *Tribune* ever since I was a kid, and the fact that it was all nonsense was exactly what made it fun to read. Thumbing through this week's edition just before dinner, I remembered those long Saturday mornings of my late childhood, when me and my dad would stop off at Value King on the way home from my piano lessons with Mrs. Wilson. There my dad would buy me two big pieces of meat lover's pizza from the café and read me the silliest stories in the *Tribune*. These days I always ended up reading the *Tribune* by myself, since Kyoko despised the phony horoscopes, UFO hoaxes, and general charlatanism the *Tribune* reveled in, but it never failed to give me something funny to think about while stocking the vitamin aisles at work.

This week's horoscope for Libras born under the waxing bloodmoon said that Hitler's ghost would visit me tomorrow at midnight to apologize for his sins. But it was the ghost of Robert Oppenheimer instead of Hitler who appeared in the bedroom that night. Oppenheimer looked frail and thin in a black pinstripe suit and gray fedora, and his glassy eyes glinted with the orange fire of the first test blast of the bomb. After a few minutes of silence, he sat down at the desk beside the bed and fanned himself with his fedora. He stared at Kyoko for a long time. She was peacefully asleep on her side, her long hair splayed across her neck and bare shoulders.

"So," Oppenheimer said.

"So," I said, in a hushed whisper, not wanting to wake Kyoko.

"Is this your wife?" he said.

"Yeah," I said.

"She's quite beautiful," he said. "What's her name?"

"Thanks," I said. "It's Kyoko."

"I see," Oppenheimer said, nodding.

"Yeah," I said. "Is there something you want me to tell her when she wakes up in the morning?"

Oppenheimer glanced out the black square of the bedroom window, where an orange sodium lamp vomited a cone of greasy light onto the neighbor's driveway.

"Tell her . . ." he said, pausing for a moment, thinking. "Tell her Thin Man failed because the spontaneous fission rate of plutonium-240 was too high to use in a gun-type bomb design."

"There's no way I'm going to remember all that," I said.

"That's fine, then," he said. "Don't worry about it."

The next night Oppenheimer appeared beside our bed about an hour before we went to sleep. Kyoko glared at him coldly as she went about her bedtime routine, but she refused to say a word to him. Or me.

Just before I turned off the lights to go to sleep, Kyoko climbed on top of me and slipped off my boxers. I grasped her hand and pointed at Oppenheimer.

"No, let him watch," she said. "He needs to see this."

For the next twenty minutes, Oppenheimer sat at the desk beside the bed and fanned himself with his fedora while we fucked. At the moment of her climax, Kyoko cried out in pleasure and yelled something in Japanese. She looked up at the ceiling and spoke the name of her great-grandfather who'd been killed by Fat Man in Nagasaki. Then she rolled onto her back and reached between her legs and pulled a glowing, red-and-black spike out of her vagina. The spike was as long as her forearm. Like a shard of cooling volcanic rock, it smoldered with heat and light. A thick string of vaginal secretion mixed with semen dripped from its needle-like tip.

Clutching the spike in her right hand, Kyoko strode naked across the room and stabbed Oppenheimer in the heart. His fedora slipped from his fingers and glided to the floor. His face twisted in pain. He didn't make a sound. Kyoko stared at him. He stared back at her. The gray plume of a miniature mushroom cloud devoured his body from the feet up.

I understand, Oppenheimer mouthed to Kyoko, as he dissolved into irradiated ash. *I understand.*

ONWARD, TO THE EARTH'S CORE!

The only thing Chris remembered about his old field goal kicker, Mike Jameson, was that he used to wear two button-up Hawaiian shirts at the same time. One right over the other. The outside one he'd always leave open, like you see guys at the beach wearing, but instead of a t-shirt or a muscle shirt underneath, he'd always have the second Hawaiian shirt there, this one buttoned up. That was back in high school. Before today Chris hadn't seen or thought about Mike Jameson in at least ten years, but then Jan came home from the supermarket and told him she saw Mike Jameson in the snack aisle, dumping hundreds of PowerBars into his cart. Apparently he needed them for the journey he was about to go on, a journey he just had to tell her all about. It worried Chris that she was talking about this instead of why it had taken her almost two hours to drive five minutes to Value King and pick up a few groceries, but he didn't say anything about that. He was trying his best to rebuild trust, exercise patience, and let go of resentments, just like Dr. Silverman had said.

"That was the exact word he used, *journey*," Jan said as she fluttered around the kitchen, putting the groceries away. Her gold-brown hair looked a little frizzed and flat, and her face and neck glowed with that warm flush of blood she used to get years ago after sex, back when the earth seemed to shift each time they touched each other, and before she started getting it from her boss over at Topine Dental, the soft-spoken, kid-loving giant, Dr. Fred. She tugged open the fridge with a squeak of sucking air and slid a container of cherry tomatoes inside. "It's actually kind of interesting when you think about it, trying to dig to the center of the earth with hand tools. It's silly and impossible in reality, but as performance art, it's actually pretty . . . inspiring."

"I guess," Chris said with a shrug, his eyes moving on their own, searching Jan's person for some clue or subconscious tell that would reveal whether or not she'd started fucking Dr. Fred again, or worse, Mike Jameson. "So what kind of PowerBars did he get," he asked, testing her, no longer trying to convince himself he was doing anything else.

After admitting to the affair three months ago, Jan had signed the two of them up for couples therapy with Dr. Rachel Silverman. Around that time Chris started reading about police interrogation techniques on his phone during his lunch breaks at the bank. That way, he was able to turn the whole thing into a game. At least that was something he knew how to deal with, like being down by three in the fourth quarter with two minutes to play. In those games all he had to do was get the ball to the fifteen yard line and let Jameson do the rest. In this one he just needed to nail down specific details, take note of the answer, and then ask the question again later, in a different way. Consistency, repetition, internal logic. By playing this game he could pretend his wife's affair was something that had nothing to do with him, just like he used to do with the numbers on the scoreboard ten years ago, under the lights on Friday nights.

With the groceries put away, Jan turned to the sink and started washing her hands, the water crashing from the faucet as a cylinder of white fuzz. Then she turned her head away from the noise and answered his question at last.

"Chocolate was the flavor he bought. Only chocolate. He said that cookies and cream has always been his favorite kind, but apparently that's just a fringe flavor that Value King doesn't carry in bulk, like they do the chocolate."

Chris nodded, absorbing the important bits of information from her answer. Bought chocolate. Cookies and cream his favorite. Fringe flavor not carried in bulk. All good bits to be shuffled and reused later.

Now Jan showed him her back and tore a single sheet off the roll of paper towels standing beside the sink. Always a single sheet, never more. Precision, a trait valued by both his wife and the dental profession at large, was a skill he never possessed as a quarterback. Size and arm strength were the only assets he brought into the huddle, genetic gifts from his parents he never had to earn. Watching her there he realized this is what you learn when you start paying attention to the edges of the picture, to the little nuggets of information that dance along the fringes of life. It's the small things that expose the truth of the stories we tell each other.

From here Chris studied the suspension-bridge outline of Jan's bra pressing through the back of her shirt, but it wasn't hooked right. The top clasp was joined to the bottom hook. Jan spun around and pressed her toes to the foot pedal of the garbage can. Slowly the steel eyelid opened, and in went the damp paper towel. A water-soft rectangle folded neatly in half.

"He's live streaming the whole thing on Twitch starting at five tonight. Since it's my day off, I thought we could check it out. Should be pretty interesting, to see how far he actually gets."

"Yeah," he said, his mind making calculations, trying to figure out the logistics of how and when she might have started fucking Mike Jameson. "Can't wait to see all the confused people commenting about his mountain of peanut butter PowerBars."

Jan squeezed his shoulder playfully as she glided past, the earthy musk of her summer sweat blurring the thoughts in his head.

"It's chocolate, babe, but nice try. Peanut butter's just a fringe flavor that Value King doesn't carry in bulk, remember?"

GOD'S THUMB

I was sixteen years old when my dad found the unmarked envelope in our mailbox. It was Easter Sunday when it came to us, a chilly day in late March, the sky a vast slab of cold granite, the air a hazy blur of icy mist.

We had just come home from mass when Dad trudged to the end of the driveway to pick up the paper. As I watched him bend over to grab the plastic-wrapped newspaper, he noticed that the door of the mailbox was hanging open. Seeing this, he walked over, peered inside, and removed an unmarked white envelope that had been placed there while we had been out.

Minutes later, me, my dad, and my little brother Dave sat down at the kitchen table and studied the unmarked envelope. It had a little lumpy bulge in it, as if someone had stuck a rotten sausage in there as a prank, and the back was all sealed up with a thick strip of clear packing tape.

Before he opened the envelope, Dad crossed himself and whispered a little prayer. I guess I wasn't the only one who sensed that something was off about it.

For as long as I could remember, Mom had always been the bible thumper of the family. While I was growing up, neither me nor my dad had ever really believed in any of that stuff, but we pretended we did because it made Mom happy. Then, shortly after she left us two years ago for her new husband Scott Carter, the rich televangelist down in Texas, Dad suddenly took up the mantle of religion in our house. I guess maybe he thought that if he finally joined her in the Jesus camp like she'd always wanted him to, she'd somehow sense it on her end and come running back to us. As for me, I joined the drama club and started acting in school plays. Since I'd been honing my acting skills my entire life, I figured I might as well do something fun with them.

Back in the kitchen, Dad opened the envelope. After a quick peek inside, he glanced up and gave me and Dave a stern look.

"Don't touch anything that comes out of this envelope," he said, his gray eyes hard and unblinking, his flinty stare scanning our faces. "You hear me?"

To this I nodded silently, but Dave didn't respond. He just stared at the envelope.

"*David?*" Dad's voice boomed, sharp and wrathful. "Did you hear what I just told you?"

At this Dave's eyes snapped up to Dad's face and then down to the table in front of him. Following this he nodded meekly, but it wasn't long until the magnetic pull of the envelope drew his gaze up once again.

Now it started to rain. A faint drumbeat of raindrops pattered against the roof overhead, and the kitchen window at my back. After a long stare at my brother, Dad finally turned the envelope over. Out came a ragged scrap of lined notebook paper and a three-inch cylinder sheathed in supermarket plastic wrap.

The moment the plastic-wrapped cylinder hit the table, Dave's hand flicked out to grab it. Just before he got there, Dad snatched it up and smacked Dave in the back of the head.

"What did I *just* tell you?" he said, leaning across the table with his head cocked to the side. "Did I not just tell you to keep your hands to yourself? Look at me when I'm talking to you."

Silent, face flushed, eyes leaking, Dave nodded his head and sat on his hands.

From here Dad leaned back and fired a quick look in my direction. I returned it with a nod, and then sat on my own hands for good measure.

Dave had ADHD. All his life he'd struggled in school, and now he was the only fourteen-year-old in the district still in seventh grade. Despite this, Mom had never allowed him to take any medication for his condition. Instead, she used to wake him up early each morning and take him to the seven a.m. mass to try to pray away his troubles. Out of all of us, Dad was the one who had opposed this practice the most, and this often led to him and Mom arguing with each other long after me and Dave had been sent to bed. But once Mom left, Dad changed his mind. Suddenly, medication was the last thing my brother needed.

Outside, the rain thickened to a downpour. Angry droplets hammered the house. A roar of thunder split the sky and rattled the glasses in the cabinet.

Hearing this, Dad looked over at Dave and pointed up at the ceiling.

"See what you did now, with that impulsiveness of yours? You pissed off the landlord."

Dave didn't answer or look up. He just sat on his hands and sniffled to himself.

"Five Our Fathers. Go. And no video games for the rest of the day."

"But that's not fair! I didn't—" Dave screeched, his eyes wild, his face a neon cherry.

"That doesn't sound like any Our Father I know."

To my surprise, Dave didn't protest again. Instead, he stared down at his lap and mumbled the prayers to himself.

Now Dad looked at the scrap of paper that had been in the envelope. Seconds later he scoffed, shook his head in disgust, and muttered to himself.

"Unbelievable, people these days. No respect for anything."

He crushed the paper in his fist and tossed it on the table. Then, very carefully, he unraveled the plastic-wrapped cylinder. Halfway through this task he suddenly stopped. As if on cue, a crash of thunder blasted outside, an explosion of sound right above our heads. From here Dad walked across the kitchen and grabbed a brown paper lunch bag from the cabinet. With his lips pinched tight into a revolted wince, he dropped the envelope, the half-unwrapped cylinder, and the crumpled scrap of paper into the bag.

"Both of you, stay where you are and don't move," Dad said, picking up the house phone hanging from the wall. The curled mouth of the paper bag was clutched in his free fist, and the knuckles on that hand had gone white.

While Dad dialed 911 on the phone, I rested a hand on Dave's warm back. He had finished reciting his punishment prayers and was now looking around the room, searching for new stimuli. To take his mind off things, I held my hand out in front of me, pointed my thumb to the ceiling, and curled my fingers into a loose hook.

"How about a thumb war?" I said, with a dancing lilt of playful competitiveness in my voice.

Upon hearing these words, he whipped his head in my direction and grabbed my hand with his sweaty fist.

"You're on," Dave said, staring intently at our linked hands, his thumb jabbing frantically at my own, the tip of his shiny pink tongue darting between his lips.

"Is this a preemptive strike? We haven't even declared war yet," I said with a laugh, holding my thumb aloft and safely out of his range. It took him a while, but soon he relaxed long enough for us to start.

Seconds later we recited the chant to start the game: "One, two, three, four, I declare a thumb war."

Ever since I taught him how to play, thumb wars had been a great way to calm Dave down. But for whatever reason, it only seemed to work when it was the two of us. If Mom or Dad ever tried to do it with him, it seemed to have the opposite effect. We first learned this when Dave was in the hospital a few years ago with a broken leg. Because of his condition he'd been injured pretty badly a number of times in the past, but this had been one of the worst. It had been so bad that even Mom admitted he needed help more immediate and potent than just prayer. In this case he'd been at a friend's house climbing trees when a contractor's truck drove by on the nearby road. Seeing the contractor's contact info stamped on the side of the truck, Dave scrabbled out onto a weak branch in order to read the words; moments later the branch snapped and Dave fell from the tree. Later that day at the hospital, when a nurse tried to check his blood pressure, Dave refused to stay still. Both Mom and Dad tried to distract him with a thumb war, but it didn't work. It just made him more upset. It wasn't until I got out of school later that day and tried a thumb war with him myself that we figured out it had to be me. Ever since then, it'd been a kind of bond between the two of us, something no one else could ever replace.

A few seconds into our thumb war I heard a knock at the door. Even though I knew how stupid and childish it was to hope that the person at the door was Mom, I couldn't help myself. Despite all she'd done to us, I still wanted her back, if only to restore us all to the way we should've been, to the way our family had been when I was a kid. When I glanced over at Dad a moment later, the surprised, hopeful look on his face told me he was thinking the same thing. After all, it did seem like something she'd do: show up unannounced on Easter Sunday, thank the Lord for bringing us back together, and ignore the fact that she was the one who had ripped us apart in the first place.

Dad held the phone between his ear and his shoulder and smoothed his silver hair over his bald spot. Then he frantically waved at me to come over to him. I broke off the thumb war with Dave, but I didn't leave him hanging. Before walking over to Dad, I lowered my chin, fixed a mock serious war-stare at him, and did my best impression of Scorpion from *Mortal Kombat*: "You and me. *Rematch. Tonight.*"

In response Dave screeched, "Get over here!" in his own imitation Scorpion voice, but one look from Dad silenced him in an instant.

Dad smacked me in the back of the head for making him wait so long.

"Pay *attention*, John. I'm over here calling and calling, and you're screwing around with your brother," he said, blowing a heavy sigh into my face. "Now listen. Take this and tell them we need the police over here for a—" he started to say, but then the knock at the door rang out again, this time more urgent. "Dammnit, just answer their questions and wait for me to come back." He shoved both the phone and the bag into my hands and started walking toward the front door.

Moments later, before I could raise the phone to my ear, Dave was up and buzzing at my side, his sweaty fingers trying to pry the paper bag from my hand.

"Get out of here," I said, pulling the wrinkled bag away from him. "Do you want to get yelled at again?"

Dave didn't seem to hear me. He just kept reaching for the bag. To get him off my back, I handed him the phone and told him to tell the 911 people that we needed the police to come to our house because of something we found in the mailbox.

Finally free from Dave's attacks, I went into the living room and crouched behind Dad's recliner. This was a nice little hiding spot where neither Dave nor Dad would be able to see what I was doing. And since I wasn't yet ready to deal with the disappointment of the person at the front door being someone other than Mom, I turned my attention to the bag in my hands.

The wrinkled brown paper unrolled without a sound. Reaching inside, my fingers found the plastic-wrapped cylinder first. Through the bunched wrapping I couldn't really see what the thing was, but it still made me feel uneasy. It felt disgustingly soft in my hands, and my earlier thought of a rotten sausage came back in an instant. At least it didn't smell like a rotten sausage.

Seconds later the plastic wrap was gone and the thing sat naked on the carpeted floor before me. It was a finger. The skin was leathery and cold and as white as heavy cream, and the nail, neatly trimmed, had been painted a tarry black. The severed end was covered with a cotton ball half-soaked in shiny red fluid, presumably blood. The whole thing looked real enough to me, but I wasn't about to check very closely.

Without the context of a hand, it was surprisingly difficult to tell which finger it was. But that question was answered for me seconds later when I reached into the bag a second time and read the scrap of notebook paper that had been slipped in the envelope with the finger.

God's thumb

Seeing this, I felt a cool wash of relief. With a note like that and a fingernail that looked like it had been painted by one of the goth kids at school, it had to be a prank. Diskin or Connors or one of my other dumbass friends from the drama club must've raided the prop closet just before spring break in order to put this together.

I gathered everything back into the bag and started walking to the front door to tell Dad that the envelope was just a prank. Two steps into the hallway, a forked branch of lightning flashed outside and knocked out the power in the house. Moments later, a blast of thunder exploded through the gray gloom, shaking the pictures on the walls. Then, before I could even grab my cell phone from my pocket to turn on the flashlight, I heard a familiar sound from down the hall: it was my mom's voice. I quickly ducked into the open bathroom on my left, crouched down on the cool tile, and held the door open a crack so I could hear what she was saying.

Mom was still the same. After less than a minute of listening to her, it was clear that she truly believed she hadn't done anything wrong by leaving us behind for a rich man. Each question Dad asked her was answered with some bullshit self-justification: it had been God's plan for her to leave us for Scott Carter, the man's wife had just died after all; all those wonderful people in his flock needed someone to help heal their shepherd; Scott Carter's indictment for wire fraud was God's way of telling her that there was nothing more she could do for the poor man, and that she had done God's work by trying to help him. The more I listened, the more foolish I felt for ever wanting her back.

But as ridiculous as she sounded, Dad was even worse. Instead of getting mad or telling her how hard things had been for us since she left, he just agreed with everything she said. Now that he'd experienced God's love for himself, he told her, he felt closer to her than ever before. And when he thought about things from her perspective, from the perspective of a lowly servant of God's will, what she had done to us made perfect sense. So in less than fifteen minutes, he had forgiven her for everything and was looking forward to putting the past behind them.

Once I heard this, I'd had enough. I didn't want to deal with either of them anytime soon, so I went back to the kitchen to check on Dave. The poor guy was probably bouncing off the walls by now.

Just before I stepped into the kitchen, I heard the howl of an ambulance siren coming up the street. In an instant I knew it was coming to our house. I had no idea what Dave had actually said to the 911 people before the power had cut out, but I just hoped it wasn't anything too far off base. He'd be in serious trouble if they thought the call was a prank.

In the kitchen I found Dave sprawled facedown on the floor. A little trickle of blood leaked from his right ear, and the smell of burnt plastic hung heavy in the air. The phone was laying on the floor next to the wall, and from where I stood, I could see that the ear piece had been charred black and partially melted, as if he'd held the phone over one of the stove's burners or something. Moments later Mom and Dad rushed down the hall and came into the living room, followed closely by two EMTs wearing light blue gloves on their hands. The EMTs pushed past me and ordered all of us to stand back and stay quiet. Dad looked at me, then at Dave, then at the paper bag in my hand. Without a word he walked up beside me and took the wrinkled bag. Since I was so overwhelmed and confused from what was happening, I didn't even think to tell him that the finger was just a prank. After finding Dave like that, it just didn't matter anymore.

The EMTs did all they could, but they weren't able to revive Dave. A few minutes after we got to the hospital, he was pronounced dead from cardiac arrest. The official explanation was that he had been struck by lightning while standing in our kitchen, and the electrical shock of this strike disrupted the rhythm of his heart, sending him into cardiac arrest. It sounded ridiculous and impossible at first, but the more I researched the doctor's explanation online, the more it made sense. Based on an article from the National Weather Service, I learned that a handful of people each year get struck by lightning while indoors. The article said this usually happens when someone is talking on a house phone during a thunderstorm, like Dave was, or when they're talking on a cell phone plugged into a charger during similar weather conditions. One unlucky guy from Kentucky even got struck while taking a shower.

Apparently, the phenomenon occurs when the bolt strikes a power line and the discharge follows the path of the wires all the way to the phone pressed to the victim's ear. When this happened in Dave's case, his 911 call was abruptly cut off; hearing the sudden hang-up, the dispatcher sent an ambulance to the address he'd given earlier in the call. That's how the EMTs arrived before we even knew anything had happened.

Once I discovered this information, I explained it all to my parents. I hoped it would help them cope with our tragedy like it had helped me, but in the weeks following Dave's death, they'd leaned so hard into their religion that they refused to accept any explanation for the accident other than divine will. Even after I showed them all my research, they still refused to believe me. So I let it go. It was such a difficult time for all of us. I couldn't put too much pressure on them.

A few months later, just before the start of my senior year of high school, a friend of mine sent me a link to a YouTube video my parents had posted the week before. Until then I didn't think my parents even knew what YouTube was, let alone how to post a video to it, but I decided to watch it anyway. I figured I owed it to them to make sure it wasn't anything they'd later regret.

The video began with a static shot of Dad sitting alone at the head of the kitchen table. He was dressed all in black and his hands, folded on the table before him, looked shriveled and arthritic and harmlessly tiny. Seeing them there it was hard to believe that they had once been the steel-palmed weapons he had used to discipline me and my brother over the years. Moments later he glanced up into the camera, but for some reason he looked different than the man I saw around the house every day. His formerly fierce falcon's stare had been replaced with the milky, distant gaze of an exhausted grandfather struggling to stay awake after Thanksgiving dinner. I guess I hadn't noticed this change because of everything that had happened to us, but now that I was really looking at him for the first time in a while, it seemed like he'd aged twenty years in only a few months.

Now he began to speak.

"Hello friends. My name is Lawrence Briggs. You can call me Larry. Earlier this year, at 12:22 p.m. on Easter Sunday, my son David was touched by God."

From here he went on to talk about what had happened to us and Dave on that day back in March, but not long into his story, I noticed something was wrong.

"And then, once we arrived home from mass, my beautiful wife and I waited at the front door and watched my son David jog to the end of the driveway to fetch the newspaper for me. He had always been such a kind, thoughtful child, never hesitating to put others before himself. As he reached the end of the driveway, he noticed that the door of our mailbox was open. Conscientious boy that he was, he walked over to close the box. But inside he found something very special. Something our Lord had sent straight to him and him alone."

As I listened to the rest of his story, I couldn't believe what I was hearing. He wasn't just stretching the truth, he was outright lying. In his version of events, Dave was the only one out of the three of us who had touched the finger. And then, at the end of his story, Dad said he had been the one who had found Dave on the floor in the kitchen, and that the finger had been clutched tightly in his son's hand. At first, I didn't understand why he would lie like that, but then I reached the end of the video. Here Mom joined him in the frame and the two of them sat down at the table together. After a short prayer, Dad walked off camera and returned a minute later holding a fist-sized cube of clear plastic. Entombed inside was the finger, and the scrap of notebook paper that identified it as God's Thumb. Then, without missing a beat, Mom took the lead.

"And this is it ladies and gentlemen," she said, grinning into the camera and gesturing down at the block sitting on the table between them. Her face was flushed and gleaming. "This is the piece of Himself that the Lord sent to our son, David, or, as all of you probably know him much better, Jesus Christ, our savior."

Following this, Mom spent the rest of the video talking about how the finger, the freak lightning strike, and Dave's ADHD proved that my brother had been the second coming of Jesus Christ.

At that point I turned the video off. I couldn't watch them delude themselves, and the 24,000 other people who had already watched the video. The whole thing was sad and disturbing.

The next day I confronted them at breakfast. It was a rainy Saturday morning. The house lay gray and quiet and chilly, and Dad had cooked scrambled eggs for the three of us. With the smell of melted cheese and fried onions filling my nose, I sat at the table and listened to the clink of silverware against plates. But I couldn't keep my mouth shut for very long.

"So I saw your video," I said, staring down at the craggy mountain range of scrambled eggs before me. Yellow juice leaked from the base of the egg-mountains and slowly flooded my plate.

Dad stopped chewing and looked across the table at me.

"Yeah? And what did you think?"

"If I'm being honest," I said, pausing for a moment, suddenly aware of how harsh my rehearsed words were going to sound. "I just—why did you have to lie like that? That's not how things happened and you know it."

"John, your father didn't—" Mom started to say, but I cut her off in a sudden burst of anger.

"You weren't even there," I said, nearly shouting. The moment these words left my mouth, I was surprised at the hatred in my voice. But I didn't take them back.

We all went quiet for a long time after this, maybe a full minute, and then Dad put down his utensils, lowered his chin, and fixed his old falcon's stare on me. It was the first time since Dave's accident that I'd seen him look like his old self.

"Now you listen to me right now. First thing. No child of mine will speak to his mother like that as long as he lives in this house. Understand?"

Mouth dry, throat clenched tight, I stared down at my plate and nodded.

"Good. Second, I will *not* be called a liar by my own son, no matter what ridiculous science-fiction nonsense he read about on the computer. Is that clear?"

Hearing these words, all my memorized research and rehearsed arguments dissolved from my head in an instant. When Dad cleared his throat a moment later, in demand of an answer, all I could do was nod.

And that was the last time we spoke about the matter.

⌒⌒

Over the next year, my parents continued to make more videos. Soon they became a viral sensation, garnering over 100,000 views on each new video. Not long after that, they officially founded their own religion. They called it God's Touch. It was focused around their delusion that the finger was a sacred piece of God's physical form, that Dave had been the second coming of Jesus Christ, and that his fourteen years of life had been spent judging humanity in preparation for the coming rapture.

As for me, I spent most of my last year of high school trying to find out who had put the fake finger in our mailbox. I talked to nearly every remaining member of the drama club, but no one would admit to the prank. As for the ten or twelve members who had graduated the year before, I used social media to get a concrete denial from all but three of them. Out of the last three, one was an economics major at Cornell and the former treasurer of the student council at our school, so I ruled her out pretty easily. The other two were solid suspects, though. Both were druggy slackers enrolled in party schools upstate. For weeks I tried to get an answer from those last two guys, but they never responded.

In spite of all this, I knew the prank didn't have to be limited to kids from the drama club at my school. Anyone could've ordered the materials off the internet and made it. All it would've taken was one weirdo who liked to mess with people for no reason. But as I ran into dead end after dead end, I started to question my memories from that Easter Sunday. Thinking back to that day, I realized I'd only looked at the finger for a few seconds at most, and even then, I hadn't examined it closely. On top of that, I had no idea how intensely my parents had studied the thing, or if they had found something I hadn't. But even with these doubts, I still couldn't come up with any plausible explanation other than a prank. It just couldn't have been anything else. And I truly believe that, even if I can't prove it.

Months later, when it came time for me to choose a college, I refused my parents' money, took out a loan, and enrolled in the North Pacific Institute of the Performing Arts, a Seattle-based school located 2,000 miles from my home and my parents' new religion back in New York. After everything that had happened, I just had to get out of Topine. Too many bad memories had been formed in that place.

Then, a few weeks into my first semester at North Pacific, Dave started appearing in my dreams. Though the dreams were almost always different, there was one that kept reappearing every now and then. In it me and Dave were back home at our house in Topine, sitting in the living room and watching TV together. Soon the power cut out and the house went black. For some reason I could still see perfectly fine in the dark, so when I looked around the living room, I saw that Dave was suddenly gone. But I wasn't scared. Because I knew that if I stood up and walked into the kitchen, my brother would be waiting for me there, ready for the rematch to our last thumb war.

GHOST BABY

Everyone in my family was a janitor, so it only made sense that I become one too. My dad was the head janitor in the school district, my mom cleaned the freshman wing at the high school, and my older brother ran things at St. Mary's hospital in town.

Two days after I graduated high school, my brother set me up with a three-to-eleven at the hospital. Each night I toiled through my eight-hour shift alone, cleaning various bodily fluids off the walls, the floor, and sometimes even the ceiling. Since my brother worked on the other side of the building, I rarely got to see him. Most of the time, I worked the entire week without saying a word to another person.

Near the beginning of my third month of work, I fell in love with one of the nurses. Her name was Sandy. Pale, thin, and delicately pretty, Sandy looked like a glass figurine brought to life. For hours each night she floated from room to room in perfect silence, a small, sad smile on her face. Everything about Sandy was quiet. Her spotless white shoes were the only shoes that didn't squeak on the waxed floors.

None of the other nurses ever said a word to Sandy. In fact, no one in the entire hospital seemed to notice Sandy at all. But I did. While I mopped the floor each night at the end of my shift, I made up stories for why Sandy always smiled in that sad way.

A few weeks later I finally worked up the nerve to talk to her. It was a cold Wednesday in October, and I was mopping the hallway near radiology. Sandy was leaning against the wall outside the MRI suite.

"Hi Sandy," I said, trying to mask the anxious warble in my voice. "Are you waiting for one of your patients?"

She stared at me for a long time. She didn't say a word.

I looked down at the floor and kept mopping. My face flushed hot with embarrassment.

"I'm sorry if I said anything wrong," I said. Then I turned around and mopped my way back to my cart, cursing my big mouth the whole way.

"Were you really talking to me?" Sandy said. Her voice was thin and distant and icy, and it was the first time I'd ever heard her make a sound.

I looked back at her and nodded.

"Oh," she said, her quiet voice rising in surprise. "Why don't you ignore me like all the others?"

"I don't know," I lied. Feeling my face flush hot again, I looked down at my boots. "Actually, that's not true. It's because of how kind you are. The way you care so much about your patients."

"Thank you for saying that," she said. "What's your name?"

I cleared my throat and looked up at her.

"Ben."

"Thank you, Ben," she said, smiling in that sad way of hers. Then she glided across the hallway and shook my hand. Her skin felt as cold as a glass of ice water. "May I ask you something?"

"Sure. Anything."

"Do you have any children?"

"No. I haven't learned how to take care of myself yet, let alone a kid," I said. "But I definitely want to have some later on, once I find the right person. What about you? Do you have any kids?"

"I love children," she said, a warm smile slicing across her thin face. "Ever since I was five years old, all I wanted to be was a mother."

"I'm sure you'll be a great mother," I said. "You're so kind."

She shook her head and stared at the floor.

"That's what everyone used to say," she said. "And then they said congratulations. And then they said that miscarriages can happen to anyone. After that, they said I should see someone. And now they don't say anything at all."

I swallowed hard. My eyes burned. I didn't know what to say.

She grasped my hand. The touch of her frigid skin sent a forest of prickling gooseflesh running up my arm.

"Will you please help me, Ben?"

Rendered stupid and powerless by the sound of my name coming out of her mouth yet again, I nodded in agreement.

Sandy led me up to the roof and told me to close my eyes. I had never even kissed a woman before, so I didn't know what was happening until she climbed on top of me. Everything about her was cold: her lips, her arms, her hands, her body. Her cold seeped into my skin and chilled the blood inside my veins. She didn't make a sound the entire time. Once it was over, we lay together and let the icy October air wash over us. Then she told me what it felt like to be dead.

"It's like when your toes go numb in the cold," she said, interlacing her fingers with mine. "You can't feel them anymore, but you know they're still there. That's how it is for me. But this," she picked up my hand and rested it on her chilly abdomen, the place where a baby would grow if she were still alive. "This will change things."

I turned my head and looked at her. She stared up at the white moon and smiled in a way I'd never seen her smile before. For a moment I thought about reminding her that she could never carry a baby inside her again, but I kept quiet. My fingers ached in the cold. My ears went numb. It was the happiest night of my life.

THE STATUE

I trudge down the center of what used to be the interstate highway. Rusting cars sit atop mountains of chewed-up asphalt. Scrub grass and beardtongue knife through long cracks in the weathered pavement. On the side of the road, fingers of dead oaks scratch at the pink sun hanging in the gold sky.

Over the crunch and scrape of my footsteps, I hear a voice within the whirl of the wind. It speaks quickly, gives clear and logical directions, wastes no time with overwrought emotion. I smile for the first time in months because this finally confirms the truth: you are not yet gone for good. I clutch your smooth hand and follow your instructions exactly.

An hour later, I find the statue of polished marble standing in the center of the highway. The statue is smaller than I imagined, only four or five feet tall, and it's right where you said it would be. It stretches its arms to the sky in a pose of joyful worship. Staring at the statue's rapturous face, I slide your hand into my rucksack, take out my rusted crowbar, and start chipping at the statue's neck. The sharp clack of steel against stone clatters down the road. I work fast, not allowing myself to forget what will happen if God catches me destroying one of His statues. But I don't stop. Over the past few months, I've come to know what this life is like without you. And that's worse than anything He can do to me.

At sunset, the statue's head rolls into the basket of my folded arm. With my heartbeat slamming in my ears, I wrap the statue's head in a thick blanket and slide it into my rucksack. Then I climb the crumbling median, cross to the other side of the highway, and start the walk home.

In the water-stained gloom of our basement shelter, I place the hand and head of your new body into the bathtub, where the rest of you has waited for weeks. I fill the bathtub with lemon juice and vinegar and salt. I prick my finger and watch beads of black-red blood drip into the spotless tub. My blood plumes through the cloudy liquid. Tiny bubbles sprout from the dissolving marble. I rest my head on the edge of the tub and listen for the sound of your breath.

WINDOW TEETH

On Tuesday morning I go to the dentist. After examining my teeth, the dentist tells me I have four cavities. She tells me I need to floss more. She tells me my flossing is inefficient. She tells me to use the string instead of the picks. I hate the string, but I don't tell her this.

At home later that night, standing in front of the bathroom mirror, I tell Kyoko what the dentist said to me.

"It's never enough for these people," I say, as the ends of my pointers go purple from the strings of floss wrapped around them. Kyoko nods in understanding and says she's never had a cavity in her life. Then she wipes and flushes the toilet and asks if she can take a look at my cavities.

For the past few months, Kyoko has suddenly become strangely worried about nearly every aspect of my health. It's nice to know that she cares, but it's definitely a change from the laissez-faire approach to my physical wellness she employed during the first time we were together more than twenty years ago. But I guess that's what happens when you get back together with your old high school girlfriend less than a year before your fortieth birthday.

Still feeling slightly defensive about my teeth thanks to my dentist's reprimand this morning, I blow an annoyed sigh and wave away Kyoko's question about looking at my cavities.

"I don't think you can just see them like that," I say.

"Then how does the dentist see them?" she says, standing up and walking out of the bathroom.

After washing her hands in the kitchen sink, Kyoko comes back into the bathroom holding the old-fashioned magnifying glass her grandfather gave her before he died.

Sitting me down on the warm toilet, she tells me to lean my head back and to open wide.

"Wow, okay, so I'm not sure if you know this," she says, "but there are like, super small people inside some of your teeth here."

"What?"

"Yeah, it's almost as if your teeth are tiny buildings with microscopic people inside them or something."

"Wait, so my teeth are full of holes?" I say, my heart thudding hard at the thought of a random tooth shattering in the middle of my next meal.

"No, they're intact, it's just that some parts are see-through, like windows."

"Jesus," I say, closing my eyes and blowing a heavy sigh onto Kyoko's magnifying glass. "What do they look like?"

"Who?"

"The people inside my teeth," I say, sliding my tongue along the front facade of my upper incisors.

Kyoko pulls back my upper lip and leans in close.

"Ummm . . . this one here looks like an apartment building, and I can see a couple that looks like us inside one of the windows. The woman especially. She looks a lot like me, but her hair is different. I really like it though. She's got this short bob kind of thing going on. It looks good on her."

"What are they doing?"

"They're standing in a bathroom of their own, brushing their teeth side by side."

"Jesus," I say, feeling worse than ever about the sorry state of my teeth. "Can they see you?"

Kyoko waves her hand in front of my face and taps one of my canines with her fingernail.

"I don't think so," she says. "It doesn't look like they can hear us either. They didn't react when I tapped on your tooth."

"Jesus," I say, shaking my head. "I don't even want to imagine how expensive it's going to be to get this fixed. And it's probably going to hurt like hell."

I stand up and start walking into the bedroom to leave a message on my dentist's voicemail, but before I can get anywhere, Kyoko pushes me back onto the toilet and pries my mouth open again.

"What are you doing now?" I say, with an acidic mix of desolation and crankiness leaking into my voice.

"Hold on, I just want to get a quick picture of this woman's hairstyle," Kyoko says. "I think I might want to try it out this weekend."

"God," I whisper to myself with a sigh. "I don't want to go back to the dentist."

On her way out of the bathroom, Kyoko stops in front of the mirror and stares at her reflection. She gathers her shoulder-length hair into her fist and holds it behind her neck. Turning her head to the left and right, she examines how she would look with the tiny woman's hairstyle. Apparently satisfied, she glances down at me and smiles. Squinting my eyes, I study her teeth for see-through windows and microscopic people. I don't find anything of the sort. Aside from the slight coffee stains, her teeth are straight, opaque, perfect. Catching me looking, she clicks her tongue and shakes her head in mock disapproval. She touches my cheek with a soft hand. She shuffles through the door and starts searching for her phone on the end table beside the bed.

While she's gone, I walk to the mirror and show myself a toothy, freakish grin. Pulling back my upper lip, I examine a couple of my teeth closely, but I don't see any microscopic people inside. The magnification of the mirror isn't strong enough, and my breath fogging up the glass doesn't help things either. After a few more seconds of staring at my teeth, I search the water-spotted edges of the bathroom counter for Kyoko's magnifying glass. I don't find it anywhere, so I pick up the small circular mirror she uses each morning to put in her contacts.

"Did you see where I put my phone?" Kyoko calls to me from the bedroom. "It's not on the end table by the bed where I thought I left it."

I close my eyes and try to think back to the last time I saw her phone, but nothing comes to mind.

"I haven't seen it, sorry K," I say. "Use mine to call it. It's on the bed near my pillow I think."

"Yeah, I guess I'll have to do that," she says.

I open my eyes and watch her pick up my phone and walk out of the bedroom.

"The unlock code is—"

"I know what it is," she says, even though I don't remember telling her.

Swiveling her circular mirror to the magnified side, I look at my teeth again. This time I see the windows she was talking about, and the tiny people inside. In one tooth-window there's an old woman with a sponge of wiry hair writing complex math equations on the walls of her apartment in blue crayon. In the next window I see a buff young bodybuilder guy with no clothes on, doing biceps curls in front of the TV in his apartment. Holding my breath to make sure I don't fog up the glass, I see that the bodybuilder guy's body is very asymmetrical: his left arm pulses thick and heavy with giant globes of muscle, while his right arm hangs at his side as limp and thin as a water-starved twig. In the next window over, I find the couple Kyoko was talking about before. They're still in their bathroom, but now the man is getting undressed and stepping into the shower. Moments after he slides the shower curtain closed, the tiny woman with the short hair quickly shuffles into their bedroom, picks up her phone, and starts typing a text to someone. As the tiny woman's husband turns on the shower, the bodybuilder guy in the next apartment stops doing curls and checks his phone. Putting down his phone, he presses his dumbbell to his naked chest and leaves his apartment. My eyes flick back to the tooth-apartment of the tiny woman with the short hair. There I see the asymmetrical bodybuilder guy enter with his dumbbell. The woman with the short hair kisses the bodybuilder guy passionately and points to the bathroom. I gulp a quivering breath and blow it out through the side of my mouth. The bodybuilder guy slowly opens the bathroom door and approaches the shower. Just as he raises the dumbbell and pulls the shower curtain back, the call box of my and Kyoko's apartment buzzes loudly from the other room. I shudder in surprise; Kyoko's mirror slips out of my hands; the metal frame of the mirror clatters against the porcelain slopes of the sink.

"Jesus," I whisper to myself, my heart hammering in my ears. As I pick up the undamaged mirror and search my mouth for the tooth-window I'd just been peering through, I turn around to ask Kyoko who the hell could be at our door at this hour of the night. But before I can say a word, she calls out to me.

"I'll get it!" she says, with a note of mischievous glee in her voice.

ON THE RIVER

On the first day of spring, the child emerges from a warm cave on a boat. The river cuts past the frozen cedar faces of his family, and in this way, he stays safe from the cold churn of the water. Inside the boat, the child sits atop a mat of green grass and fresh berries. The colors are beautiful: bright red, shiny black, marbled blue. He reaches for the most exciting berry of them all, the red. It feels soft and spongy between his fingers. He closes his small hand and squeezes. Sticky red juice runs down his arm. He mashes the mangled flesh into his mouth and licks his fingers clean.

᷒᷒᷒ ᷒᷒᷒

At the end of the summer, the river narrows to a thin creek choked with sharp rocks. Gripping the tiller firmly, the back of his hand baked red by the sun, the boy steers his boat carefully down the creek. Soon he sees a young woman picking wildflowers on the shore up ahead. Thin white robes cling to the curves of the woman's body; a cool summer breeze ruffles her ebony hair. She's the most beautiful thing the boy has ever seen, so he waves his free hand above his head and calls out to her. She glances at the boy for a moment and then turns her attention back to the flowers. His face burns with blood and he tries to look away, but he can't. His body doesn't let him. The young woman's beauty is an elemental force as powerful as gravity's pull. The boy's boat slips down the creek. He loosens his grasp on the tiller. A black crag scrapes across the bow, gouging away the curves of his father's mouth, the pits of his mother's eyes.

⌒‿‿⌒

By autumn, the man sees many more women on the shore. One sits in the grass and offers breadcrumbs to the starlings and the cardinals and the sparrows and the crows. Another strums an acoustic guitar and sings a beautiful song in a language the man doesn't understand. A third writes in a small book and watches a gold leaf spiral to the ground. Stranded in his boat on the creek, the man falls in love with all of the women on the shore. To win their affection, he offers them the freshest, most delicious berries in his boat. He compliments their songs, their beauty, their creativity, their kindness. But the man's efforts are clumsy and transparent. Some of the women glance at him for a moment and look away, but most don't acknowledge his existence. After weeks of failure, the man lays in his boat and stares at the gray slab of the sky. Soon his boat slams into a rock. Then another. And a third. Instead of patching the hull, the man crosses his arms and listens to the splintering crunch of the bow. He draws a deep breath. The prickly smell of snow hangs in the chilly air.

On the coldest day of the winter, the old man's boat gets stuck in a lake of ice. There are no strawberries left, so he no longer has a choice of what to eat. Bitter and angry, the old man sucks on a frozen blueberry and curses everything and everyone in the entire wretched world. By the next morning, the old man can no longer feel the cold. Soon the young woman he saw at the end of the summer appears beside his boat. She's more beautiful than he remembers. Her ebony hair hangs to her waist; her white robes glow with a soft pink light; a pair of skin-sheathed wings lay folded on her back. The young woman smiles at the old man and offers her hand, but the old man's poisonous resentment takes hold of him, and he severs her arm with a blade of splintered wood. Pink light explodes from the stump of the young woman's shoulder; she disappears without a sound. When she reappears the next day, her body made whole again, the old man is as cold and stiff as the keel of his trapped boat.

RICHIE'S VACATION

Richie was sitting in his mail truck, eating a spicy chicken sandwich, when he got a text from his mom that said his old best friend from middle school was dead. Richie hadn't been friends with Emmitt since the summer after eighth grade, and the two hadn't seen each other since the day of their high school graduation over seven years ago, but from that moment on, Richie couldn't stop thinking about Emmitt for the rest of the day.

That night, after Richie finished his route, he skipped dinner, threw his aching body onto his bed, and blasted album after album of experimental black metal.

By midnight, Richie was still wide awake. Thoughts about death and the transience of his own existence churned endlessly in his head. For the first time in his life, Richie understood that he too could die at any moment. With this thought in mind, he decided he was done wasting his life doing miserable shit that he hates, like working six days a week for the post office. So he stuffed some clothes into his gym bag, grabbed his phone and charger off the dresser, and walked out the door.

At the ATM near his apartment, Richie withdrew five hundred dollars from his account. Since all he ever did each week was work, he had a good chunk of savings squirreled away for a rainy day.

For the next forty minutes, Richie drove north with no destination in mind. He gripped the steering wheel tightly as the road cut through rolling fields of grass and low-lying swampland. Gnarled oaks and ancient elms flicked past like specters of a future leaden with suffering. At some point during the drive, a feral cat slinked across the street, stopped in the opposite lane, and stared at Richie with shimmering green eyes.

Just before one a.m., Richie rented a room at a hotel off Route 23 called The Quartzite Inn. Stepping into room fourteen, Richie slumped down on the bed and stared up at the ceiling. It hung low and was painted the same color as vanilla bean ice cream. Its dimpled texture resembled buttered popcorn. With his swirling thoughts finally quieted by the thrill of his spontaneous trip, he realized he had not eaten anything since his lunch break at Wendy's almost fourteen hours ago. So he locked his room and walked across the street to the twenty-four-hour diner he'd spotted while parking his car.

A neon red *Open* sign glowed in the window of the diner as Richie walked through the front door and sat down at the counter. Aside from an elderly woman slumped behind a cash register near the door, a hard brown blob of dried maple syrup was Richie's only company in the entire place.

At the end of the counter sat a bell and a white scrap of paper. *Ring for Service*. Moments after Richie rang the bell, a cook with a scarred face walked out of the kitchen and asked Richie for his order.

"Do you have a menu I can look at?" Richie said, trying to not stare at the cook's craggy face, which resembled the surface of an asteroid-pocked exoplanet.

The cook gave Richie a drooping smile and shook his head. At this distance Richie could see that the cook's left eye was fake, and that the scars on his face spread down his neck and extended all the way to the backs of his hands.

"We got diner food, man," the cook said, with a friendly upward flick of his chin. "Anything you want, you got it. It's not like I got any other shit to do right now, you know?"

"Yeah," Richie said. He drew a deep breath and smelled grilled sausage, melted butter, and fresh bacon. He looked down at the counter in front of him and saw the dried blob of maple syrup. "Can you do chocolate chip pancakes with sausage and bacon?"

The cook flashed his lopsided smile and nodded.

"Oh yeah. Coming right up," the cook said. He smiled at Richie one more time and then disappeared into the kitchen.

Once Richie had finished with his food, the cook came out of the kitchen once again.

"So how was it, man?"

Richie smiled at the cook as the post-meal warmth washed over him.

"I think that might have been the best meal I've ever had in my entire life."

"That's what I like to hear," the cook said, grinning. "You need anything else?"

"No, I think I'm all set, thanks."

"Alright, I'll get your bill, and then you can pay Janice over there on your way out. You have a good one, man."

The cook picked up Richie's dirty plates and started walking away.

"Actually, can I ask you a question?" Richie said to the cook's back.

The cook turned around and pointed at the scars on his face.

"They're from an accident a couple of years ago. I got burned."

"I'm sorry," Richie said. "I'm sure people ask you about it all the time."

"No, you're good. It was pretty goddamn awful at the time, but I don't mind talking about it now. It's a crazy story if you want to hear it."

Richie looked at the old woman sitting behind the cash register.

"Is that okay? You're not going to get in trouble or anything will you?"

The cook burst into laughter and shook his head. He had the wet, wheezing laughter of a heavy smoker, just like all of Richie's coworkers at the post office.

"Don't worry about her. She's not the boss. The boss loves me. I'm her all-time favorite employee."

"Okay."

The cook put down Richie's plates and sat at the counter.

"Alright. So basically, for the first twenty years of my life, I was a member of this cult called the Light of the Second Storm. Me and my little brother were born into it, but that was only because of our parents. When our parents first met in the early nineties, they were both hardcore drug addicts. You know, shooting heroin, living on the street, panhandling, stealing, all that shit. They were trash. Then at some point they met this asshole named Father Elijah who said he knew how to save them from death or hell or whatever. According to him, he had discovered a way to transfer little pieces of Jesus' soul into other people's bodies, and whenever he did that, Jesus' power was supposed to heal them up just like that. So he tried this with my parents. I don't know what the trial was like at the time because I wasn't there, but in the story my parents told me and my brother, he did something amazing and they got clean right there. No methadone or withdrawals or anything. Just clean. Like a miracle from heaven.

"Once that happened, they were hooked. They were all in. Now fast forward twenty years. I'm nineteen, and my little brother Paul is eighteen. By then Father Elijah had developed his soul-swapping shit into a whole bunch of tests that took years to complete. He called them the Trial of the Second Soul. And for the kids like me and Paul who had been born into all this, the final test of the trial was supposed to take place just before your twentieth birthday. So on the night before my twentieth birthday, Father Elijah took me, my little brother Paul, and my parents out into the fields on the edge of his farm down in Topine. Now my birthday is in January, so it's fucking freezing out there. We're all tromping through the snow and the mud and it's awful. So finally we get out to this big open field with a little cluster of trees in it. In the middle of these trees there's a small clearing, and in the middle of the clearing there's this square plastic table. I swear to

125

God. It was like one of those tables you buy at Home Depot for sixty bucks. So we see this table standing there. On top of the table is a roll of gauze, a metal jug of water with a lid on it, and a Tupperware container filled with those long matches you use to light old fireplaces.

"So like I said, that night was supposed to be my final test in the Trial of the Second Soul. For that test I was supposed to stand still and watch in silence as the person I loved most in my life offered up their body to Jesus. This was done by lighting one of their fingers on fire. According to Father Elijah, if the soul of the person on trial was spotless like it was supposed to be, then the flames would quickly die out and the host of the fire wouldn't feel any pain. But if the soul of the person on trial was blackened with filth, then the flames would engulf the host's body and burn away the evil of the pigs and the whores and the unbelievers. And since I was the one on trial, Father Elijah lit Paul's finger on fire, because he was the person I loved most in my life.

"So we started the trial. I stood on one side of the table and Paul stood on the other. Then Father Elijah wrapped Paul's pinky in gauze and picked up one of the long matches and lit it with his lighter. When he touched the flame to the end of Paul's pinky, a big ball of smoke blew up in our faces and both of Paul's hands caught on fire. I still don't know why that happened, but either way, the fire ran up Paul's arms and got into his robe, the stupid goddamn robe we had to wear for the trial, and the whole thing just went up in flames. It was unreal. Paul stayed quiet for a few seconds, maybe two or three, and then he started screaming. But since we were all so brainwashed by Father Elijah's bullshit, no one did anything. We all just looked at Father Elijah. About two seconds later, that chickenshit turned around and ran as fast as he could back to the farmhouse. So I grabbed the jug of water off the table and threw it on Paul. But it turned out that it wasn't water in the jug, it was actually lighter fluid. And since my nose was all stuffed up from the cold, I couldn't smell the lighter fluid when I picked up the jug. So the second I threw that shit on him, a giant fireball exploded in my face and engulfed me too. By then our parents finally woke up and tried to help us out. My dad tackled me and Paul to the ground and rolled us in the snow while my mom ran back to the farmhouse and called 911. But because of the remote location Father Elijah had taken us to, the EMT's couldn't get to us in time, and Paul died out there a few minutes after I turned twenty years old."

"Oh my God," Richie said. "That's so crazy. I'm so sorry that happened."

"Thanks," the cook said. "Yeah, Paul was my boy. He was so funny. That kid could make me laugh about anything."

"He sounds like a great guy," Richie said. "But how can you be so—I mean you seem to be so happy in general. If something like that had happened to me, I don't think I'd be able to get out of bed ever again."

"It ain't easy, man," the cook said, shaking his head. "But then again, I was never too big on any of that self-pity shit anyway. I got too much I want to do with my life, you know? And on top of that, I'm not too sad about it because Paul's still here with me right now. Without the skin they harvested from his lower body, I wouldn't have made it either. So each time I start to get sad, I try to think of what he would say if he was looking at me right now. Knowing him, I'm pretty sure he'd be cracking some joke about the doctors sewing his ball sack onto my face in order to save my life. And then he gets me all over again."

Richie and the cook laughed.

"Yeah," Richie said. But his laughter and good cheer quickly dissolved away when he imagined how painful and terrifying Paul's final minutes must have been.

"Anyway," the cook said, clearing his throat. He grabbed Richie's plates once again and stood up. "You need anything else tonight, man?"

"No, that's enough," Richie said, slumping over the counter. He mopped his sweaty forehead with a wad of napkins and mashed the heels of his hands into his eye sockets.

"Alright, I'll be back with your check in a minute, and then you can pay Janice on your way out."

"Thanks," Richie said.

After paying his bill, Richie returned to his hotel room and slept for twelve hours. When he finally woke up, the clock beside the bed read 2:16 p.m. Instead of checking his phone for notifications, he lay in bed and stared at the dimpled ceiling. Then he turned onto his side and watched a glowing square of gold sunlight inch across the blue carpet. Nothing happened for a long time. He thought about turning on the TV or searching for porn or Googling one of his ex-girlfriends from college, but he didn't do any of those things. Instead, he closed his eyes and tried to go to sleep again. It didn't work. He was wide awake. He was bored. There was nothing more he wanted to do.

THE GIRL WHO WAS A DOORWAY

Days after Miranda began middle school, strangers started thanking her. Always it was boys who did this, boys she'd never met and who were not in her classes, boys with jumbled teeth and missing fingers, boys with limps and tics and roaring coughs. Without saying why, they thanked her in supermarkets and in restaurants, at the park and in the library.

On a cool Sunday morning near the end of September, while reading a Nancy Drew mystery in her back yard, Miranda saw a handsome teenage boy suddenly erupt from the ground behind the big sugar maple in the middle of the yard. Brown crumbs of dirt and green frizzles of grass clung to the boy's long black hair as he looked around in a daze. Moments later he jumped the fence and ran away, but he soon returned and thanked her like all the others. Before he could run away again, Miranda asked him what she had done to deserve his thanks. He grinned and revealed a nubby ridge of naked pink gums in the place where his three front teeth were supposed to be.

"You gave me a second chance," he lisped.

From here he told her about his alcoholic parents and hopeless life, and how everything would be different now thanks to her.

Following this incident, the thank-yous continued for another two years; then, a few days before winter break of seventh grade, they stopped just as abruptly as they had begun.

～～

Years later, not long after turning fifteen, Miranda felt a pain churning in the soft place just north of her belly button. Cold and fibrous, crackling with electricity, the pain curled its tendrils around every part of her life. No longer could she act on her own; her pain had to be consulted first. Sometimes the pain let up for a bit, but it never went away. Always it swirled, dragging her forever inward.

The pain made it hard to sleep. Lying awake in the middle of the night, the dark house creaking around her, Miranda imagined her life in the future. She thought of the people she might care for as a nurse, the animals she might help as a vet, the lives she might touch as a social worker. In this way her pain would fade away and she would finally fall asleep.

Soon a solid ball of tissue formed under her skin near the source of the pain. Weeks passed and the ball shrank and hardened, then morphed into a narrow vertical ridge running from belly button to sternum. Turning dry and crusty, the skin above the ridge began to swell and crack. Days later the ridge became a wound, leaking and itchy, smelling of cool earth, a reptilian pupil etched into her flesh.

Miranda kept her wound a secret. She didn't want her parents or anyone else worrying about it, not with so many others around the world suffering so much worse than her. To protect her secret, she took to the internet and researched how to clean and dress an open wound.

Upon returning to school in September, the men started watching her. Wet and hungry, their darting eyes followed her through the hallways, the lunchrooms, the parking lots, and the classrooms. They all seemed instinctively drawn to her wound, to the earthy smell of it, to the heat it belched in blurry waves. And it wasn't just boys her own age who were drawn to her. Teachers, administrators, coaches, and custodians all stared at her in ways they wouldn't dare with other students. Suddenly, it seemed that she couldn't go anywhere without the head of every man turning in her direction.

Eventually Miranda began accepting some of the many dates she was asked out on. Even with her wound and the pain swirling behind it, she couldn't come up with one good reason to say no to the most attractive boys in school.

Although the dates usually started good, they all ended the same way: the boys always wanted to see her wound. But moments after peeling back her bandage they would disappear, her bones crunching and unhinging to take them inside, her taut skin stretching like a balloon to swallow them whole. By the fourth or fifth date, when a handsome boy with long black hair started talking about his alcoholic parents and hopeless life, Miranda finally understood what was happening. From this point forward she decided to start using her ability to improve as many lives as she could.

The first two years of transports were a success. She didn't even charge a fee for her services. After that, things went bad. Her pain turned crippling. Some mornings she woke up and couldn't feel her legs for the rest of the day. Other days she suffered through migraines powerful enough to split the sidewalk. Not long after, she started vomiting up the missing parts her body took from the boys: fingers, toes, jewel-like teeth; pinkish chunks of hearts and lungs.

In addition to her worsening health, the men started harassing her wherever she went. They bellowed at her on the street and begged for a chance to fix their wasted lives. They followed her home from school and started showing up at her house at all hours of the day and night. Soon they were pounding on her front door, throwing rocks at her bedroom window, and sending death threats to her parents.

Miranda began to fear for her life, and the lives of her parents. Days later she woke in the middle of the night to a strange man carefully peeling away her bandage; but when the police arrived twenty minutes later, they dismissed her complaint in an instant and sternly interrogated her and her parents about the boys who had gone missing over the past two years.

Following this incident, Miranda understood that her parents would never be safe with her around. The men would never stop; it was not in their nature. So, a few minutes after her parents went to bed the next night, Miranda wrote a note telling them how much she loved them, and how sorry she was for bringing so much trouble into their lives. She left the note on the kitchen table and went back into her room. Laying down on her bed, Miranda peeled the bandage from her wound and slowly thrust her hands into the opening in her flesh. Her bones crunched and unhinged. Her skin stretched and unraveled. A powerful force pulled her deep inside herself, into a swirling vortex of marbled light, and she was gone.

LUNCH BREAK

At 10:06 a.m., a serrated electronic buzz tore through the silent air of Carl's bedroom. Carl twitched awake; he clambered off his bed; he fumbled with the screeching clock and switched off the alarm. After rubbing a sharp crust from the corner of his left eye, he walked to his dresser and slipped on a pair of wrinkled jeans and a plain white t-shirt with a yellowed sweat stain clinging to the right armpit.

Once finished with his morning shit, Carl walked into the kitchen and turned on the TV. There he clicked over to ESPN and ate four bowls of Berry-Berry Kix. While Carl chomped on his cereal like a cow, the soft sugary spheres mashing between his molars, an ESPN anchor talked about an NHL playoff game between the Blues and the Wild. When the show went to commercial, Carl picked up the remote and switched to HBO and watched the first fifteen minutes of *Goldeneye*.

Twenty minutes later, Carl trudged down to the basement and stepped onto the treadmill. During his warm-up he clicked into the on-demand menu and selected *Goldeneye* from the HBO section. He fast-forwarded to the spot he left off from at breakfast and played the movie from there. For the main portion of his workout, he ran five miles in thirty-six minutes. The treadmill belt screamed for the last seven minutes of the run, so he had to turn the volume on the TV to the max in order to hear what Pierce Brosnan was saying. But since his parents were already at work, Carl didn't have to worry about the roar and crackle of the TV disrupting their morning routine. This was a relief. After they had been generous enough to let him move back home rent-free while he tried to get started on a new career in engineering, the last thing he wanted to do was cause them any more trouble.

He stepped off the treadmill at 12:49 p.m. and stopped the movie at the point where Alec Trevelyan revealed himself to be Janis. Crystalline sweat trickled down Carl's face and neck. His legs ached with a cold pulsing burn.

Upstairs, Carl stepped into the shower and stood in the spiny spray of the hissing water. The beat of the water against his face felt like two hands slowly massaging his skin, their invisible fingertips kneading his cheeks and back like raw dough. Once finished in the shower, he grabbed his math notebook and his calculus textbook and folded the two books under his left arm. He left the house at 1:37 p.m. and forgot to lock the front door.

⌒――⌒

Carl reached the Topine business district in ten minutes and pulled into his usual spot near the back of the CVS parking lot. The July heat hung around his shoulders like a dead bear; the sun smoldered above as a blurry smear of liquid gold. Trudging across the parking lot, Carl found a stray shopping cart marooned in the gray ocean of pavement; he steered the clattering cart to the entrance of the CVS in which he worked and pushed it into the bodies of the other carts standing just inside the door.

Time crawled like a snail. Carl rang up an old woman with wrap-around medical sunglasses five different times in one hour. Each transaction consisted of a single item of small monetary value: a can of soup (chicken and wild rice); a store-brand lipstick (some dull shade of pink); a small candy bar (a one-hundred-calorie Milky Way); a six-ounce bottle of dish soap (neon-blue Dawn); and a can of cat food (ocean whitefish in gravy).

Standing behind the front counter, Carl's ankles and knees ached with a dull, starry pain. To take his mind off his throbbing legs, he theorized possible trades the Mets could make before the deadline to bolster their bullpen depth or the bottom half of the batting order. He believed these two weaknesses would need to be addressed before the team could make a second-half run at the wild card.

Three hours into his shift, the old woman with the medical sunglasses stepped back into the store and tried to return the five small items she had purchased earlier. The can of soup was now empty and lidless and slick with yellow liquid, and the candy bar was nothing more than a mashed stick of crushed chocolate and sticky caramel. Carl bellowed across the counter and tried to explain that the store did not accept returns for food items, consumed or otherwise, but the woman refused to listen and demanded to speak to a manager. Obliging the woman, Carl paged Diane to the front and stepped aside as she explained the store's return policy for twenty minutes. Carl watched this scene with a detached fascination. For the first time since he had signed up to take summer classes at Topine Community College, he felt proud of himself for doing extra work on his new engineering degree that would hopefully one day rescue him from this place.

Carl took his lunch break at eight p.m. After trudging across the parking lot, he climbed into his black Honda sedan and thrust the key into the ignition and left it hanging there. Slipping his headphones into his ears, he pressed play on his Spotify playlist. Craig Armstrong's sugary strings hummed their sweet stretchy melt, their goopy rhythmic drip. From here Carl clicked on the overhead light and opened his calc book to page one-eleven and laid the heavy textbook across his lap. He knew that by burning this light he risked walking out of the store at ten p.m. to a dead battery, but he did it anyway. For whatever reason, bad things like that had never happened to him before.

For the next twenty minutes he worked on the review exercises for section 1.4. These problems presented him with the task of factoring fractional exponents out of complex polynomials, but every few seconds his eyelids slipped closed and erased his memory of the work he had done up to that point. After another six minutes of failure, he gave up and drove to the gas station next to Value King to get gas.

With his gas tank refilled, Carl returned to the plaza and parked in his usual spot. He knew he wouldn't be able to stay awake if he tried to do more schoolwork, so he grabbed his keys and climbed out of the car. He checked the time on his phone. It was 8:23 p.m.

"Just an hour and a half and then I can get out of here," he whispered to himself.

Carl walked into the store and tried to clock in. He was too early; the system refused him with a screeching tone. So he emptied the garbage cans behind the front counter and carried the three bags to the backroom. Before taking the garbage out to the dumpster, Carl locked his phone in his employee locker and cleaned the microwave in the break room with a series of disinfectant wipes. He was the only person in the entire store who ever did this; if he didn't do it, it would never get done.

Two minutes later he stepped outside and trudged to the dumpster sitting at the edge of the rear parking lot. The woody fingers of overhanging tree branches tickled the backs of his hands as he lifted the lid of the dumpster and tossed in the air-bloated garbage bags. The wet, fruity stench of garbage swirled around his head, leaked into his nose, and burned the back of his throat. He blasted a few honking coughs and let the dumpster's ribbed lid crash against its steel body.

As he walked back to the store, he heard a panicked scream emerge from the woods behind the dumpster. He froze in place and held his breath and listened. For a long time he heard nothing but the whirl of the gusting wind and the blare of a distant car alarm. He listened for another minute or two and then exhaled and resumed his walk back to the store. Just before he stepped inside, he heard the voice again. It was a woman; this time he was sure of it. And she was screaming for help.

A hot crackle of electricity flashed up Carl's spine. With no memory of turning around, he found himself charging past the dumpster and surging through the woods toward the source of the woman's voice. In the dark he caught his toe on a hooked root and sprawled to the ground. A sharp rock cut across his left knee; a streak of stony dirt bisected the twin curves of his lips. Scrabbling to his feet, he wiped the mud from his mouth and strode toward the pin of light burning up ahead.

Soon he emerged into the back yard of a small white house with a dying garden fenced inside a wobbly pen of green chicken wire. An overhead sodium lamp coughed sickly yellow light onto the grass as Carl hunched low to the ground and shuffled toward the back door of the house. A child's neon-pink sled lay cracked in half on the lawn in front of the garden, and each half of the sled was filled with a thick black cake of dirt. Three silver candy wrappers shuddered in the grass beside the two halves of the sled. Approaching the house, Carl heard another panicked whimper; at this sound he paused and surveyed the rest of the scene. The back door of the house hung open; the window just above the silver knob was shattered; the open door revealed a dim hallway.

Carl drew a quivering breath and climbed the three steps leading to the back door of the house. The old wooden stairs bowed under his light weight; shards of broken glass crunched beneath his Nike running shoes. Standing at the threshold of the open door, Carl held his breath and listened. Here he heard something that sounded like quiet crying or heavy breathing, but he couldn't tell where the sound was coming from.

Carl glanced down the dim hallway. Near the end of the hallway, he saw a wet, streaky stain that looked like a bloody drag mark. Reaching into his pocket for his phone, he hissed a curse word when his fingers closed on empty air: he had locked his phone in his employee locker back in the store. With no way to call the police and no one around to help, he gulped a quivering breath and forced himself through the doorway.

The floorboards creaked as Carl crept down the hallway. Before he could investigate the frightening stain on the floor, he came upon a blind right turn. Carefully peering around the corner, he found a short, dead-end passage leading to a room with an open door. This small box of a hallway stretched less than twenty feet long and measured no more than seven feet wide. Once he was sure it was empty, he took a few steps down this section of the corridor and glanced inside the room at the end. Staring back at him was a dark, windowless bathroom with an ugly yellow shower curtain. Moments after he pulled back the shower curtain to check for the intruder, the floorboards groaned behind him. Turning around, Carl saw a huge man with sunken eyes, a silver beard, and a six-inch kitchen knife clutched in his hand. Without a word the man lunged forward and slashed a deep horizontal gash across the front of Carl's right shoulder. Carl's arm blazed with searing pain as he tried to spin away, but he slammed into the wall on his left and trapped himself in the small hallway leading to the bathroom. Carl clawed at the two framed pictures hanging on the walls beside him, but they crashed to the floor like icicles shattering and slid out of his reach. In response to the intruder's attack, Carl held his hands in front of his body like a martial artist from an action movie and bobbed to the left and right, but the huge man took no notice and inched forward with the tensed liquid smoothness of a stalking lion. An instant later Carl faked left and then lunged right as quickly as he could, grabbing for the knife, but the man was more agile than he looked, and he slid backward and slashed Carl's right palm at the base of the knuckles and laid open the flesh there. Carl made no sound at this injury outside of a sharp, hissing intake of breath. With nowhere else to go, Carl hopped backward and stood in front of the bathroom doorway. It was in this moment that the trapped-animal panic took over his mind and his body began to tremble. The huge man stepped backward and watched Carl for a moment, as if he was about to flee the scene completely, but then he lunged forward with the knife held at his hip. Carl thrashed his body to the right but there was no room there and his slashed shoulder crashed against the wall and exploded in pain; in the next instant, a wet choking sound burst from his throat as the knife pierced his left side just below the ribs and tore five inches into his trunk. Carl's trembling hands cradled the wound as blood bubbled at the site of penetration and soaked warm and sticky into his work shirt that had not been washed in three weeks. In seconds all strength and heat and feeling drained from Carl's body and he fell backward through the doorway of the dark bathroom and the back of his head smashed against the wooden door and sent it swinging open. Moments later Carl heard the hard clack of the doorknob smacking against the wall, a sharp clear crack of brass against tile, and then the man, the knife, the hallway, the bathroom, and the world, disappeared.

MEETING THE HUSBAND

When you first met Christina in a musty corner of the bookstore, a shining bar of sunlight resting on her tattooed wrist, you didn't know she was married. Finally learning your lesson from the last one, you remembered to look at her hand this time; but she had rings on every finger, not just the important one. Later, as your tongue toured her body, you found many small cuts and scars in her pretty skin. And on each shoulder, pressed into the taut shelf of muscle near her collarbone, you saw some imprints that looked like bite marks.

Moments before coming for the first time, she slapped you across the face without warning. Seconds before the second time, she bit you on the shoulder and left a bruise. In the afterglow of the third, she sighed happily and talked about the forest: the lazy flutter of falling leaves, the fruity musk of rotting wood, the hot knives of sunlight cleaving the muddy trail.

When not fucking, you and Christina hiked the woods outside town. During these times she asked you many questions about your life and your childhood and the women you had loved and fucked in the past, but she never said anything about herself. Although you sometimes wanted to, you didn't ask her any questions of your own. Things were going good in your life for once, and you didn't want to fuck everything up again.

Then, on a steamy summer morning two months after you met, as you walked the rocky trail and breathed her spiky sweat, Christina said her husband wanted to meet you. She said she had a special arrangement with him and out of respect she could not deny him certain requests. Hearing these words, you felt a length of steel cable coil around your stomach. You felt betrayed, tricked, and played for a fool. Unlike her, you had always tried to keep pain and pleasure separate. In the past these things had mixed as well as ice cream and olives. But you couldn't endure the other parts of your life without her touch. So you agreed to meet her husband.

A week later you hiked the woods with them. Prior to the hike, they arrived in separate cars. As he climbed out of his Ford pickup, you saw that her husband was not the man you had expected to meet. Instead of curly hair, sandals, khakis, and a soul patch, you saw a bald head, muddy jeans, work boots, and a wiry beard. To your surprise, he seemed to be genuinely excited to meet you. His handshake was hearty and his hands were soft and while he had your hand in his grip, he introduced himself as Marty. From here he leaned in close and grinned at you strangely; but before you could think of something to say, he crushed your hand in a savage grip and rolled your knuckles as if trying to break every bone in your hand. Your face flushed from this bright shock of pain, and when you tried to pull your hand away, he squeezed harder. Then you heard Christina's voice and your hand was suddenly free. By the time she turned around and looked in your direction, Marty was standing at the tree line six feet to your right, running a finger along a spongy vein on the back of a star-shaped leaf. Now Christina came close, close enough for you to smell the oils in her hair. You tried to smile at her, but the knuckles on your palm throbbed with a sour ache, and this hurt bent your lips into a crooked grimace of pain.

Christina led the hike and pointed out her favorite things in the forest. After a while, she suddenly went quiet and shuffled out ahead by herself. You quickened your stride and matched her pace without a thought, but then something hard and rubbery smashed down on your Achilles tendon and scoured the skin raw there. Your heel popped out of your shoe and you fell to one knee; the pain pulsed sharp and thick, like the crack of your father's belt across your back, but you didn't make a sound. It was around this time that you began to understand what was happening. Seconds later a cool shadow swallowed your crouched body and Marty's hands slipped under your arms. You rose to your feet without effort. The pressure under your arms eased. You looked down the trail and saw Christina walking alone up ahead, wholly unaware of what had happened, her tanned legs scissoring the black dirt. Too afraid to say a word to either of them, you crouched to fix your shoe. An instant later you felt the searing burn of a thin knife slicing open the back of your arm. To keep yourself from crying out, you pressed your eyes closed and bit the inside of your cheek. Some time passed and a bird sang from somewhere nearby, somewhere close to the ground; the animal seemed to be saying, *teacher, teacher,*

teacher. You could not feel any blood yet but you knew it was there, meandering over your elbow. Staring at your shoes, the ground and your feet seemed very far away. Somehow, your arms bridged this distance and you slipped your heel back into your shoe. Now you looked down the trail once more, trying to locate Christina's shape, but she was gone. Seeing this, you sprang to your feet and ran away. You ran and ran and ran. The pain came fast and hard, from all the distant regions of your body, and after a time, once it was clear you were free from them, it even started to feel good. Then, as you climbed into your car, sticky red blood dripping from your fingers, you understood that she had been right. Some pain can be a pleasure after all.

A TEXT FROM ZOEY

Just after seven I'm cruising down 17 on my way home from the warehouse, headbanging to some Nile, when I get a text from Zoey telling me to pick up some baby formula at Target. Apparently our little Char-char has already sucked down the whole big-ass tub of Enfamil we got last month and now we need some more. Sliding into the right lane I think of my infant daughter and hope this isn't a sign of things to come with her, but it wouldn't surprise me if it was, knowing my bottomless pit of a stomach. I know Zo would flip her shit if Char-char grew up to be a big old fat-ass like me, but as long as she's happy and healthy I say who cares. Funny how all of a sudden it's practically a crime these days to be a little bit bigger than everyone else. But if we're not supposed to eat all this so-called crap, then why does it all taste so good? Whatever the reason, it's a hell of a lot better than the raw granola, gluten-free, open-range garbage Zo cooks at home.

As I drop my phone onto the empty passenger seat beside me, I realize I've already passed the last exit for Target and will now have to bite the bullet on price by getting the stuff somewhere else. So off goes my Nile and up goes my blood pressure and a few minutes later I pull into the parking lot of the CVS next to Eighteen Wheels, that trucker diner that's always open no matter what time it is.

Inside the CVS, standing in the baby aisle, that tight little burning sensation crackling away in my chest, I suddenly realize I have no idea what kind of Enfamil I'm supposed to get. I know we need the infant category, but outside of that, I have no clue of which of the five choices in front of me is the right one. Worried about screwing things up again, I track down a shaggy-haired kid wearing a navy blue CVS polo and ask him. Before he can answer I look at the prices and realize I don't have enough cash for any of them, because each one is at least ten dollars more expensive than it is at Target. The kid mumbles something I can't make out and points at the most expensive tub before trudging away, his shoulders slumped halfway down to his waist. Watching him walk away I cringe at the thought of working here. Everyone always coming and going, zipping past on the highway, and then here you are, stuck in the same place all the time. Thinking about it like that it sounds just like my life at the warehouse: all that shipping and receiving, freight going in and out, nothing ever changing except that burning feeling in my chest getting hotter every day.

I lean forward and check the label on the tub the kid pointed at. Apparently this type of Enfamil is filled with all kinds of special chemicals that boost BRAIN BUILDING and IMMUNE HEALTH. Seeing this I read the label over and over, hoping the words will knock something loose in my head, some memory of having seen this label before, but nothing comes. After a minute of gaping, I say fuck it. I snap a picture of the tub, send it to Zo, and ask her if it's the right one.

Just before I reach the candy aisle Zo responds with a series of impatient texts. Their lack of proper grammar tells me just how pissed off she is right now.

> *yea thats it*
> *what in gods name is taking so long*
> *get it here asap*
> *char is flipping out*
> *jesus thats expensive*
> *why the hell are you not getting it in target like i said*

The flame in my chest expands as I read her last text, and suddenly my entire face is slicked with cold sweat. Thinking about where I could've messed up, I realize that she must've seen the CVS label on the shelf at the bottom of the picture I sent her. To buy myself some time I type an excuse about Target being out of stock, and then I turn off my phone and stuff the giant thing into my back pocket. I'll deal with her later. First I have to find a way to get an extra ten dollars for this formula. With all our credit cards maxed out due to baby expenses, I'm going to have to get creative.

Moments later, as I walk out of CVS on my way back to the car, the flickering neon sign of the trucker diner next door catches my eye. Before I know what I'm doing, I'm walking through the door of the diner and sitting at the counter next to a big guy with a handlebar mustache, a camo FORD baseball hat, and a black Metallica t-shirt.

Sitting on the counter in front of him is a steaming cup of black coffee and a dinner plate. Half of an open-face tuna melt sits in the center of his plate; the slab of mayo-drenched tuna stands nearly two inches high, while a partially melted slice of cheddar sweats on top. A single breath fills my nose with the hazelnut scent of his coffee, the toasted bread smell of his sandwich, and the melted-cheese aroma of the cheddar on top. Thinking of the tasteless garbage that awaits me at home, it takes all of my willpower to keep my hands away from his plate.

Before I can tear my gaze from his sandwich, the guy suddenly turns and looks at me.

"You okay there, hoss?" he says.

When I finally look up I see that his lips are cracked into a friendly, knowing smile. From the threads of gray in his mustache and the fine lines fanning out from the corners of his eyes, I can tell that he's at least twenty years older than me.

"You hungry?" he says, gesturing with his head at the tuna melt on his plate. "Didn't even touch that half. It's yours if you want it."

To hide my embarrassment of getting caught ogling his dinner, I ignore his offer and introduce myself. Then I tell him about Char-char, about the formula I have to get, and about the ten dollars I need in order to buy it.

He nods and grins in all the right places while listening to my story. Every now and then he takes a sip of his coffee. Once I finish talking, he introduces himself as Floyd. Then he leans back with a groan and reaches into his back pocket. His metal stool creaks under the pressure.

"Well, that's quite a pickle you've got there, Tom, but I don't think it'll be too tough for us to get you straightened out."

Floyd leans forward and smacks a pack of playing cards down on the counter between us.

"Your daddy ever teach you how to play war?"

"Sure, but I don't really have time to—" I start to say, shaking my head. My phone feels heavy and deadly in my back pocket, like a live grenade that could blow up at any moment.

"One game. Winner gets the ten spot," he says, interrupting me. "And whatever he wants off the menu. A hard-working family man such as yourself deserves a break every now and then, don't you think? Or a nice, hearty meal at the very least. Work yourself too hard and you're liable to drop dead one morning. And *then* where would your little girl be?"

As I listen to his words, my tired heart starts pounding. For the first time in as long as I can remember, the burning in my chest goes away. But then I remember Zo's series of angry texts, and the burning comes back, hotter than before.

"Thanks for the offer, but I really can't. Like I said, Zo and my girl are waiting for me at home, and Zo is already pissed off as it is, so I'll be lucky if they're even still there when I get back."

Floyd studies my face for a few seconds and then turns back to his coffee and shrugs.

"Suit yourself, hoss," he says, taking a long sip from his mug. "I know it's none of my business, but from where I'm sitting, it looks like some missing baby formula is the least of your problems."

With these words hanging in the air, I turn around and look out the diner window. The sky behind the CVS blazes a brilliant neon pink, and the cars on the highway are now nothing more than pairs of yellow-brown dots crawling through the evening gloom. By the time I turn back to the counter, a ten-dollar bill sits in the place where the playing cards used to be. I take the money and steal one last look at Floyd's tuna melt before thanking him for his help and walking to the door.

"Good luck to you," he says, as the door glides closed behind me.

⌒﹏⌒

Thirty minutes later I walk into my kitchen with the tub of Enfamil tucked under my arm. In an instant my head is enveloped by a gross smell worse than boiled cabbage mixed with rain-soaked shoes. Looking to my left I see that the kitchen table is all set and ready to go for dinner, and in the middle is a giant bowl filled with some ungodly concoction of steamed spinach, cubes of diced tofu, and red kidney beans. Sitting at the head of the table with Char-char cradled in her arms, Zo glares at me with a look of wrathful anger. Then, while Char-char is distracted by the tub of Enfamil under my arm, Zo mouths some words at me.

We. Need. To. Talk.
Now.

At this I smack the Enfamil down on the counter and take a deep breath. Slowly, the burning sensation in my chest fizzles out.

I turn around and face my wife.

"Yes," I say, my voice calm and free of fear. "Yes, we do."

HOWDY STRANGER, THIS IS HOWSER

SwimmersEar69: hello cutie pie

SwimmersEar69: one of us is in deep trouble

RussConklin15: lol sweet screenname who's this?

SwimmersEar69: IM DETECTIVE JOHN KIMBALL

RussConklin15: wait are you serious?

SwimmersEar69: YES

SwimmersEar69: IM DECTITIVE JOHN kIMBALL

RussConklin15: sorry but there's no way you're a cop

RussConklin15: my dad is the head manager at circuit city and he barely knows what instant messenger is so there's no way you're a cop

SwimmersEar69: IM DETCETIVE JOhN KIMBALL!!!!!!!!!! !!! !!!111!!!!!!!!!!! !!!11111111 1111111111111111111!!!!!!!1111 ASDIFHP W8EYFA

RussConklin15: whoa ok sorry calm down

SwimmersEar69 has signed off

SwimmersEar69 has signed on

SwimmersEar69: hello cutie pie

SwimmersEar69: one of us is in DEEEEEEEEEEEEP troubleeeeeeeeeeeeeeeeee

RussConklin15: seriously who is this

SwimmersEar69: DECTIVE JOHN KIMBALL!!!!!!

RussConklin15: is that your real name? why does that sound so familiar

SwimmersEar69: Because im dECTETIVE JOHN KIMBALL

RussConklin15: wait isn't that Arnold's name in kindergarden cop?

SwimmersEar69: I LIKE YOU RUSSEL

SwimmersEar69: YOU AND I ARE GOING TO HANG OUT UNTIL THE END OF TIMEEEEEEEEEEEEEEEEEEEEEEEEEEEEEEEEEEEEEEEEEEEEEEEEEEEEEEEEEEEEEEE

RussConklin15: lol yeah that's definitely from kindergarden cop

RussConklin15: me and my older sister have been saying that line to each other ever since we saw it on starz over the weekend

SwimmersEar69: whats a matter

RussConklin15: what?

SwimmersEar69: i SAID wHATS THE MATTER

RussConklin15: oh

RussConklin15: it's just that I don't mind talking about movies or whatever because I'm a big Arnold fan too but I kind of need to know who you are

RussConklin15: the rents don't like me talking to people online who I don't know in real life

RussConklin15: I had some messed up stuff happen to me last year when I was a freshman so I don't use instant messenger with people I don't know in real life sorry

SwimmersEar69: FUCK YOU, ASSHOLE

SwimmersEar69 has signed off

155

SwimmersEar69 has signed on

SwimmersEar69: howdy stranger, this is howser

RussConklin15: ok I know for a fact that's from total recall but that's messed up

RussConklin15: don't call me an asshole when I didn't do anything wrong

RussConklin15: you're the one who started talking to me and I don't even know who you are

SwimmersEar69: im ben richards, the butcher of bakersfield

RussConklin15: that's not your real name

RussConklin15: that's Arnold's name from the running man

RussConklin15: I just watched that two weeks ago right after this kid in my social studies class made this poster about

RussConklin15: wait

RussConklin15: is this jake skinner from Topine high in New York?

SwimmersEar69: nope

SwimmersEar69: im the world famous comedian, Arnold Brownschweiger

RussConklin15: come on this is jake isn't it

RussConklin15: you sit behind me in Nelson's social studies class

RussConklin15: you made that poster of the top ten Arnold Schwarzenegger movies just before everything happened

SwimmersEar69: you mean before my older brother blew his head off with a glock in our bedroom?????????????? ???

SwimmersEar69: is that the everything your talking about russel????????????????????????

RussConklin15: I'm so sorry I didn't mean anything

SwimmersEar69: lmfao its fine russ your a good dude

SwimmersEar69: you got to go easy on that hair gel tho

SwimmersEar69: most days your head looks like a fuckin hornets nest or some shit

SwimmersEar69: and thats no good

SwimmersEar69: Arnie would not approve

RussConklin15: lol yeah it gets pretty messed up on the way to school because the gel takes so long to dry

SwimmersEar69: and I think you need to start hitting the gym too

SwimmersEar69: got to lift those weights until your biceps cum

RussConklin15: lol wtf?

SwimmersEar69: Arnold says that in pumping iron

SwimmersEar69: I guess thats one Arnold movie you haven't seen

RussConklin15: yeah no I haven't seen that one

SwimmersEar69: it's a documentary about Arnolds weightlifting days

SwimmersEar69: at some point he says that the burning feeling he gets from lifting weights is as good as cumming

SwimmersEar69: its awesome and hilarious just like the man himself

RussConklin15: lol what

RussConklin15: that's crazy that he actually said something like that

SwimmersEar69: yeah its pretty great

RussConklin15: yeah

RussConklin15: so how have you been doing

RussConklin15: you haven't been in school since your brother

SwimmersEar69: since my brother what

RussConklin15: sorry I didn't mean anything bad

SwimmersEar69: since my brother what russ??????? ????????????

SwimmersEar69: you need to type the fuckin words russ

SwimmersEar69: because if you and everybody else keeps dancing around the truth with this hippy dippy pussy wussy bullshit it will never be real

SwimmersEar69: and if its never real nobody will ever be able to get past it

SwimmersEar69: so you need to go ahead and type the words russy wussy

RussConklin15: I'm really sorry I shouldn't have said anything

SwimmersEar69: too late fucker

SwimmersEar69: you did say something so now you need to TYPE THE FUCKIN WORDS!!!!!!1

SwimmersEar69: its easy just do it like this

SwimmersEar69: how are you doing jake? You havent been at school since YOUR BROTHER KEITH BLEW HIS BRAINS OUT WITH A GLOCK

SwimmersEar69: ARE YOU OK? DOES IT BOTHER YOU THAT ALL YOU SMELL WHEN YOU WALK PAST YOUR BEDROOM IS SHIT MIXED WITH GUNPOWDER?

SwimmersEar69: DOES IT MAKE YOU SAD THAT YOU CAN STILL SMELL THAT SMELL EVEN AFTER YOUR BEDROOM WAS CLEANED UP BY A PROFESSIONAL CRIMESCENE CLEANUP SERVICE?

SwimmersEar69: DO YOU GET ALL EMO AND SHIT WHEN YOUR MOM TREATS YOU LIKE A FOUR YEAR OLD WHO CANT DEAL WITH SHIT BY TAKING YOU OUT TO THE MOVIES ON THE DAY THE PROFESSIONAL CRIMESCENE CLEANUP SERVICE PARKS THEIR VAN IN FRONT OF YOUR HOUSE AND CLEANS YOUR BROTHERS BLOOD AND SKULL FRAGMENTS OFF THE WALL NEXT TO YOUR BED?

SwimmersEar69: DOES THAT BOTHER YOU JAKEY WAKEY?

SwimmersEar69: see its easy

SwimmersEar69: now its your turn

SwimmersEar69: just do it like that

RussConklin15: I'm so sorry jake but I'm not going to say that

SwimmersEar69: well i guess i was right about you then

SwimmersEar69: you are a fuckin pussy who uses too much hair gel

SwimmersEar69: i guess ill see you around russy mussy pussy wussy

SwimmersEar69: or not because im driving into NYC tomorrow morning to meet with the same guy who sold my brother his gun

SwimmersEar69: id use keiths glock but the po-pos or whoever took it away

SwimmersEar69: so have a nice life russ

RussConklin15: wait but why does it smell like shit I thought you said your brother shot himself

SwimmersEar69: because at the moment of death the bowels release

SwimmersEar69: so he shit his pants just after he blew his head off

159

SwimmersEar69: and since the gunpowder and the shit were released at the same time the smells mixed together

SwimmersEar69: and that was the first thing i smelled when i opened our bedroom door before i even saw his body or the blood on the wall or anything else

SwimmersEar69: and now every time i try to go up to the second floor of our house all i smell is my dead brothers shit mixed with gunpowder

SwimmersEar69: so i cant go up there anymore

SwimmersEar69: since then ive been trying to sleep on the couch in the living room downstairs but its been really hard

SwimmersEar69: now most nights i just watch Arnold movies or play n64

SwimmersEar69: i finally beat turok 2 a few days ago tho and it was fuckin awsome

SwimmersEar69: the last two levels are so crazy and long and confusing but their so amazing

SwimmersEar69: you got to get that game if you have an n64 i swear to god russy play fuckin turok

SwimmersEar69: but just 2 not the original

SwimmersEar69: 2 is so much better than 1

RussConklin15: yeah that's what I heard

RussConklin15: I want it so bad but my rents won't buy it for me

RussConklin15: they say it's too violent

SwimmersEar69: yeah its pretty fuckin violent

SwimmersEar69: theres this crazy gun called the cerebral bore that shoots a pod that drills into the enemies head and then it blows up and their head blows up

SwimmersEar69: its almost as awesome as the end of commando when Arnold throws a steam pipe thru bennets chest and tells him to let off some steam

RussConklin15: lol wow that sounds pretty crazy

RussConklin15: but yeah my rents would kill me if they ever saw that so it's no wonder why they won't get it for me

RussConklin15: I guess I'll just have to wait until senior year when I finally turn 17 and I can buy it myself

SwimmersEar69: yeah its violent as hell but the thing that adults don't get is that its silly too

SwimmersEar69: like Arnolds movies

SwimmersEar69: im pretty sure keith blew his head off because he felt as shitty as i do right now not because he watched too many Arnold movies or played too much doom or turok or whatever

RussConklin15: yeah maybe

RussConklin15: but what about turok 3?

SwimmersEar69: i havent played it russy it just came out

RussConklin15: but if you drive to NYC and buy a gun and shoot yourself like your brother did you'll never get to play it and that would really suck

RussConklin15: and Terminator 3 also

RussConklin15: Terminator 2 was one of the best movies ever so I'm sure they'll make another one

RussConklin15: don't you want to be around to see that?

SwimmersEar69: damn

SwimmersEar69: you got me there

SwimmersEar69: but im so tired russ

SwimmersEar69: im so fuckin tired

SwimmersEar69: you know what i did that night after i beat turok?

RussConklin15: no tell me

SwimmersEar69: it was after 2 in the morning and everyone else was asleep so i walked out the front door of my house and laid down in the middle of the street and asked my brother to send a car to come and run me over

RussConklin15: wow

RussConklin15: I'm so sorry

SwimmersEar69: you need to stop with the sorry sorry shit russ

SwimmersEar69: just be real for fucks sake

RussConklin15: ok

RussConklin15: well in that case I'm glad your brother didn't listen to you that night

SwimmersEar69: HE WAS LISTENING DUMBASS!!!!!! 111!!!!!!!!!!!!!!!

RussConklin15: sorry

SwimmersEar69: SAY SORRY AGAIN

SwimmersEar69: SAY SORRY ONE MORE MOTHERFUCKIN TIME!!!!!!!!!!!!!!!11111111111!!

SwimmersEar69: lmfao yeah thats not Arnold but Samuel L in pulp fiction is pretty classic too

RussConklin15: lol wow you scared the crap out of me

RussConklin15: yeah that's a good movie too

RussConklin15: but if your brother was listening, what did he say?

SwimmersEar69: he didnt really say much in the word sense

SwimmersEar69: he just kind of materialized in the road beside me out of nowhere

SwimmersEar69: it was def weird and at first i didnt really know what to say but then i started talking about how i finally beat the lair of the blind ones in turok after we had been stuck on that level for like a year and then i just kept talking and after a while things went right back to how they were last summer before he started up with his community college shit and got all depressed and everything

SwimmersEar69: it was pretty sweet

RussConklin15: that does sound cool

SwimmersEar69: yeah

SwimmersEar69: and after that we started reminiscing about this day last summer when me and him drove around for a couple hours and went out to this amazing chinese food buffet next to genos pizza place in that little strip mall on the edge of town

SwimmersEar69: that was a great day

RussConklin15: wow yeah that does sound like an amazing day

SwimmersEar69: yeah

SwimmersEar69: but then i forgot he was dead and i turned to the side to look at him and i saw that nobody was there

SwimmersEar69: and that was when i finally realized i was totally alone in the world and that the only person who ever understood me was gone forever so i decided right then to drive into the city to meet with the gun guy

SwimmersEar69: because who gives a shit right russ?

SwimmersEar69: i dont have my license yet but keith had been letting me drive his car since last summer so i already know how to drive it

SwimmersEar69: and its not like ive got anything better to do with the rest of my life

SwimmersEar69: lmfao im pretty sure it was going to be all downhill from here anyway

SwimmersEar69: so be good buddy

SwimmersEar69: and go easy on that hair gel

RussConklin15: but what if you did have something better to do?

SwimmersEar69: thanks russ but im good

SwimmersEar69: i finally feel ok with everything now that ive decided to do this so im not going to bail on that now

RussConklin15: well then what if you just push the NYC plan back a few days so we can hangout and play some turok this weekend or something

RussConklin15: after talking to you tonight I kind of wish we had been friends earlier because you're pretty cool

RussConklin15: and I would say sorry for being a dick and never talking to you even though I sit right in front of you in Nelson's class but I know you hate it when I say sorry so I won't

SwimmersEar69: haha thanks russy

RussConklin15: so will you do it jake?

RussConklin15: you can sleep over my house on friday and then once my rents go to bed we can play some turok and watch that Arnold movie you were telling me about with that weird line Arnold says

RussConklin15: and my rents are really heavy sleepers so we can prob sneak outside and hangout with your bro too

RussConklin15: after hearing you talk about him he sounds really cool and I really want to meet him now

RussConklin15: if that's ok with you I mean

SwimmersEar69: jesus christ

SwimmersEar69: you are such a fuckin nerd

RussConklin15: lol yeah that's what everyone says about me

RussConklin15: so what do you say?

RussConklin15: do you want to sleep over my house on friday?

SwimmersEar69: my god you are such a nerd

RussConklin15: so you'll come over on friday?

SwimmersEar69: shit

SwimmersEar69: i dont know

SwimmersEar69: im so tired russ

RussConklin15: ok you can go to bed soon but if you're going to sleep over I just have to tell my mom by thursday morning so she can buy extra food for dinner on friday

RussConklin15: so can you tell me before bed tomorrow night?

SwimmersEar69: jesus your such a goddamn nerd

RussConklin15: can you jake?

SwimmersEar69: yeah fine ill think about it christ almighty

RussConklin15: cool, sounds good!

RussConklin15: talk to you tomorrow!

RussConklin15: g'night jake!

SwimmersEar69: my god your annoying

SwimmersEar69: but whatever

SwimmersEar69: talk to you tomorrow night i guess

SwimmersEar69 has signed off

NOTES FROM THE WAR

Note #1

I lay on my back on the forest floor, in the exact place they first arrived seven years ago. Aching from the hike and my gnawing hunger, I stretch my body into a five-point star and stare through the trees at the sky. As the air grows cold and the sunset dissolves into the red-baked black of the night, I close my eyes and picture their faces of polished silver. Their thin, long bodies laced with gold circuitry. Then, just before melting into sleep, I try to summon them into my dreams once again.

Please come back to us.

Don't leave us here alone with each other.

Note #2

While foraging in the woods for food, you find a skeleton near a cork elm ringed with wood lilies. The bones are arranged into an X. A jawless skull of polished silver sits at the center of the X and stares up through the trees. Clumps of thick clouds hang bloated and black in the sky, ready to dump radioactive rain on the world. Without thinking, you reach out to touch the gleaming skull. But you stop when you remember what your father said on the day he left for the war.

Never touch anything strange in the woods.

Note #3

At the beginning of the sixth year of the war, me and my sister saw a soldier fall out of the sky. From our bedroom window we watched him glide through the air like a leaf and crash through the roof of our barn. We woke up mother and followed her outside. The soldier's parachute was caught in the roof; he hung limp and unconscious from the lines. A white cloth stained with engine oil had been sewn onto his flight suit, covering the flag of our bitter enemies to the north. I pointed at the cloth and started to speak, but Mother spit on the floor and tore the cloth and grabbed the old ax off the wall.

Take your sister back to the house and lock the door.

Note #4

Lying in bed, the rough covers pulled up to your chin, you ask your mother if they're ever coming back. You ask her what happened when they first landed in the woods. You ask her why they tried to help us when they didn't even know who we were. Then, without waiting for her answer, you tell her what the Miller twins said about them last week: that their star had transformed into a red giant, that they talk to us only in our dreams, that their ships are made of a special gold that's not heavy.

That's why everybody keeps fighting and no one wants to be friends with them, you say, *because it's easier to kill them and take their stuff when they're not our friends.*

Your mother looks at you for a long time and then closes your favorite book about precious metals. Her eyes are blue. She looks very tired.

I don't know about that.

I don't really know about any of this stuff anymore.

There's no more grape jam in the house, so me and Theo eat dry toast for breakfast. The crumbs are hard and sharp and tiny, and we flick them at each other while we eat. Mom stands by the window and stares at the dirt road at the edge of the yard. While she's distracted, I bite my crust into a boomerang and throw it at Theo's neck. His face scrunches up like a raisin. He starts to cry. Some jeeps from our army roar down the road toward the Miller Farm, where the enemy soldier crashed through the barn two days ago. Mom thinks we don't know about the soldier, but we do. After she put us to bed last night, we heard her whispering about him on the phone with Mrs. Miller.

Once the jeeps are gone, Mom picks up the kitchen phone and starts dialing. Halfway through the number she stops, clicks the hang-up button, and starts dialing again. She stops again. She clicks the hang-up button over and over. She screams louder than Theo's crying and slams the phone against the wall a few times. Theo stops crying and looks at me. I look at him and then out the window to the road. The dust kicked up by the jeeps hangs in the hazy air. A rope of black smoke rises from the Miller Farm. Before I can ask Mom what's going on, someone pounds hard on the front door. Mom presses her finger to her lips for quiet and ushers us into the basement. Just before closing the door, she holds my face in her hands and stares at me.

Keep the lights off and find a good hiding spot and stay there.

Stay quiet no matter what.

Everything is going to be okay.

Note #6

Your escape from your unit complete, you reach the woods outside town just before dawn. There you sit on a wall of stacked stone and crunch into the last fresh apple from your pack. Once finished, you stretch your neck in a slow circle and watch the sunrise. Oaks and elms creak in the early morning breeze. Feathers of pink flame leak through the serrated teardrops of the leaves. In the east, a glittering star emerges from behind the sun. Streaking across the sky, it falls in a shallow arc and then pauses. From where you're sitting, the star seems to be hovering directly overhead, but you can't tell for sure. Then it begins to descend. It flies straight down, growing larger with each passing moment, its gold body glinting in the morning light.

STROLL

For what would be her final performance piece before the cancer claimed her life, the artist slathered her hairless body with the darkest substance on earth, a highly toxic, ultra-black paint composed of carbon nanotubes. Once the paint had dried, she slipped on a pair of dollar-store sunglasses and walked naked through the streets of her Brooklyn neighborhood, her paint-glazed skin absorbing 99.96% of the light it came in contact with.

During the brunch hour, diners held up their phones and tried to take pictures of the knife-slash black hole that was the artist's body. But she walked on without a word, crisscrossing Brooklyn for hours, ignoring the cacophonous noise of the bustling city in which she had cried and smoked and fucked for the past forty-eight and a half years.

At sunset her legs went numb and she experienced the sensation of floating above the pavement like a spirit, the sharp October cold chilling the fibrous ligaments linking her bones. But on she walked, staring into the depthless voids of her feet, her body slowly dissolving into the blue-black darkness of the encroaching night.

In the morning, bars of gold sunlight sliced between the buildings and stretched across the sidewalk. Speed-walking pedestrians sucked fruit-flavored smoke from electronic cigarettes. A pair of dollar-store sunglasses lay unscratched in the center of the street. The artist's body was never found.

BROTHER TIMOTHY GOES
TO THE BATTING CAGES

For Brother Timothy's first session of exposure therapy, his therapist Jerry took him to the batting cages. There Jerry handed Brother Timothy an aluminum bat with no grip and a filthy red helmet whose white ear pads were stained black with ancient sweat. Looking at the helmet, Brother Timothy told Jerry that the world of filth is the world of pigs and whores and eternal damnation, and that the only path to salvation passes through Father Elijah's cleansing tongue, but Jerry just laughed and thumped Brother Timothy on the shoulder.

"Father Elijah's fuckin dead, brother, you ain't gotta worry about him anymore. Now put that helmet on your head and pull down on those ear flaps till everything's nice and tight. Go on. It ain't gonna bite you."

When Brother Timothy hesitated, Jerry twisted the helmet onto his head and gave it a good smack. Though he felt no pain, Brother Timothy shuddered in fear. After struggling for so many years to complete Father Elijah's Trial of the Second Soul, he didn't really understand what pain was anymore.

"What'd I tell you?" Jerry said with a grin. He held his arms out at his sides and looked around. "You're still here ain't you?"

Before Brother Timothy could answer, Jerry steered him into station one of the batting cages (slow softball, 40 mph), and showed him the right way to stand beside the square of black electrical tape on the ground. Just as the red eye of the pitching machine flicked on, Jerry scooted out the door.

The first pitch whizzed past Brother Timothy's face like a bullet from an ATF agent's rifle. He screamed in terror and fell to the ground. The aluminum bat clattered against the concrete and rolled to the other side of the cage.

"That was a close one, brother!" Jerry said, from behind the cedar lattice. "But you see that? You're still breathing, ain't you?"

Brother Timothy sat on the concrete and shielded his head with his arms. Another pitch screamed past and thumped against the backstop. Brother Timothy drew a quivering breath. He looked at Jerry and nodded.

"That's what I'm talking about, Tim," Jerry said, his voice dropping to an intimate whisper. "*You can do this.* I wouldn't have brought you here if I didn't think you were ready to get out into the real world. You ain't gotta worry about that cult ever again. They can't hurt you anymore."

Brother Timothy cleared his mind of all thought. He took another breath. He nodded again.

"There's my man," Jerry said. "You got six pitches left, brother, and then you're out. Just hang in there. You ain't gotta do nothing."

But Brother Timothy had done nothing for too long, and because of that nothing, everyone he had ever loved was now either dead or in prison. So he dashed to the other side of the cage, picked up his bat, and waited for the next pitch to whiz by. Then he jogged back to the left side of the cage and stood next to the square of black tape on the ground. He looked back at Jerry to make sure he was standing the right way. Jerry motioned for him to take a half step away from the square. Brother Timothy adjusted his stance. Another softball screamed by, smacked into the backstop, and rolled down the sloped concrete. Jerry opened his mouth to say something, but he stopped himself and nodded. Brother Timothy turned back to the pitching machine and stared into the glowing red eye. Gripping his bat tightly, he watched as the mechanical arm scooped up a yellowed softball and let fly the final pitch.

ALL THE THINGS YOU DO

Vic was working the tail end of a three-to-close at Geno's Third, the pizza place near his house where he worked nights. Since there was only one customer left in the place, a lone guy going to town on the three slices of chicken, bacon, ranch he'd just sat down with in a corner booth, Vic decided to ask his boss, Little Joey, about his newest TV obsession, the classic HBO crime series *The Wire*. On Vic's recommendation, Little Joey had started watching *The Wire* a few weeks ago, just after finishing *The Sopranos* for the third time.

"So what'd you think of season four?" Vic said, wiping down the front counter with a rag. *The Wire* was Vic's favorite show of all time, and it was the show that, in a past lifetime, had inspired Vic to try to become a television script writer by enrolling in the screenwriting program at Topine Community College. "Did you get a chance to finish the last episode this morning?"

Little Joey stood hunched over a sudsy sink on Vic's right, scrubbing dried tomato sauce off the spinning blade of a pizza cutter. In response to Vic's question Little Joey threw his head back to the ceiling and huffed out a few exaggerated breaths, as if the question was too much for his heart to handle.

"Bro, Vic, *buddy*, who do you think you're—yes I finished the fucking thing! It was amazing! That thing my guy said to McNulty at the end there, about how your life is all the shit you do while you're waiting around for moments that'll never happen? Oooof. I felt that. That's the story of *my* life. You know what I'm saying?"

"Yeah, I hear that," Vic said, even though he couldn't imagine Little Joey wanting to do anything with his life outside of working here in his dad's pizza place.

"What's that guy's name, again?" Little Joey said. "The detective, the sharp guy who said that to McNulty."

"That's Freamon, Lester Freamon," the lone customer said from his booth without looking up. "That's my guy. Best character in the show." The customer dabbed at his lips with a napkin, picked up his second slice, and took a huge, chomping bite.

Hearing this, Little Joey exploded out from behind the sink and smacked the counter with his huge, soapy, catcher's mitt of a hand.

"Yes! Lester Freamon. Lester! What a great character," Little Joey said, turning to Vic just in time to mist his face with a spray of excited spittle. At twenty-four years old, just over a year older than Vic, Little Joey had the energy and enthusiasm of a two-hundred-fifty-pound middle schooler. He was also the main reason Vic still worked here, more than a year after his son Sal had been born and he had been forced to drop out of Topine CC's screenwriting program. Sure, Vic loved his son more than anything he'd ever loved in his life, but neither Sal nor Sal's mother Pauline had ever even heard of *The Wire*, so it felt good to spend time with someone who shared a love for his former passion. For a few hours every week, Little Joey's enthusiasm for prestige television helped Vic hold on to a part of himself that had been slowly rotting away with each passing day. "Lester Freamon. He's so sharp. Nothing gets past that guy."

"Seriously. That's my guy right there," the customer said, still focusing all his attention on his slices.

Little Joey waited a few seconds in anticipation of the customer's next comment, but once he saw that that was all he was going to get from the guy, he grabbed a ratty rag from the supply closet, dried his hands, and draped the grime-stained cloth over his mountainous shoulder. Then he walked out from behind the counter and turned around the OPEN sign hanging on the door. On his way back to the kitchen he tapped his red knuckles on the edge of the customer's table.

"We're going to be closing her up soon buddy, but take as long as you need. We ain't going anywhere for a little bit," he said to the guy. Then he slid in behind Vic and grabbed something from under the counter.

"I'm going to have a smoke out back, so don't burn the place down, *capiche*?" he said to Vic with a big grin. He was holding the wooden baseball bat his dad Big Joey had stashed behind the counter last summer after a pair of high school idiots had gone barreling through the kitchen and out the back door. "Lester Freamon. Man. What was it again? Life is all the things you do while you're waiting around for moments that'll never happen? Oooof. I feel that, buddy. I'll be back."

Vic picked up his rag and started erasing Little Joey's soapy handprint from the counter. Moments later the lone customer stood up, wrapped his last slice in a cocoon of white napkins, and slid the grease-darkened triangle into the hip pocket of his baggy jeans. Then the customer reached into his other pocket and pulled out a snub-nosed revolver and walked up to the counter. Vic watched a dark amoeba of grease soak through the stonewashed denim of the customer's jeans, but he didn't have much time to pay attention to this because in the next moment the customer raised the gun and pointed it at Vic's chest. The customer gave Vic a long stare to make sure they understood each other. Once satisfied, he lowered the gun to his hip and ordered Vic, in a sticky whisper more frightening than any shout, to open the register.

With the gun in such a vulnerable and unsecured position, Vic wondered if this was one of those special moments Lester Freamon had been talking about at the end of season four of *The Wire*: a rare opportunity to change the course of your life by doing something brave and extraordinary, like grabbing the gun out of the hand of an armed criminal. But as Vic thought about this, he realized he no longer cared whether he was extraordinary or not. Thanks to the clarity of this life-threatening situation, he finally admitted to himself that he liked the low expectations of Loserville, that he enjoyed the comfort of mediocrity, and that he had used his son as a shield to protect himself from the shame of failing at a dream he never had the determination to achieve in the first place. Because in order to fulfill your dreams, you have to *try*. And in the current state of his life, working two minimum-wage jobs, still living at home with his parents, his one-year-old son the only bright spot in his life, *trying* was just too much work for too little return. Sure, he could try to lunge for the gun and foil this robbery and become a big hero who Little Joey might someday install as the manager of one of his family's other restaurants, a turn of events that would earn Vic enough money to quit his other job and move his family out of his parents' house and maybe even give him the chance to go back to Topine CC to start writing scripts again, but in order to make any of that happen, he'd actually have to start *trying* again. And that wasn't worth the effort. So instead, Vic stood very still and waited for Lester Freamon's life-changing moment to float off into the stuffy, grease-fogged air of the kitchen.

Seconds later it did just that: angered by Vic's long silence, the customer tightened his grip on the gun and pointed it at Vic's chest once again.

Now that the pressure of Lester Freamon's life-changing moment was gone, Vic nodded at the customer and quietly popped open the register. As he did this, he spotted Little Joey out of the corner of his eye. The back door of the restaurant was propped open, and through it he saw Little Joey standing in the rear parking lot with a lit cigarette clamped between his lips. He was taking a big, jerky practice swing with the wooden baseball bat, and from the way he moved, it was clear he hadn't heard Vic open the register.

"Lift up the drawer and gimme the big bills underneath," the customer said, the right corner of his lips shiny with pizza grease. He darted his head left and right, checking the front door and the kitchen for movement. "I don't want any of that small shit. Just the twenties, fifties, and hundreds."

Vic did as he was told. There were only five fifties and one twenty that someone had put under the drawer by mistake, but he handed it all over anyway.

The customer took the money without looking at it and jammed the wad of bills into his pocket without the pizza.

"Now close the register quietly and keep your mouth shut. You say anything to fat boy out there and you're dead, got it?"

Vic nodded and stayed very still.

Moments later Little Joey yelled something outside.

"Oh! Rendazzo hits a deep fly ball down the right field line, and it's outta here! The Mets win it in the bottom of the tenth! Mets win! Mets win!"

The customer gave Vic one last menacing look and then he slipped through the front door and melted into the night.

For the next few minutes, Vic stood motionless behind the front counter and stared at the beige wallpaper on the opposite wall. In his head he tried to picture his son's face, but the image wouldn't appear. His mind was blank.

The back door slammed shut. Little Joey came up behind Vic and put the baseball bat back in its place under the counter. When Vic felt Little Joey's huge, heavy, hot hand thump down on his shoulder, he spoke.

"We just got robbed," Vic said.

"You're shitting me," Little Joey said.

Vic shook his head.

"The guy," he said, pointing to the booth where the lone customer had been sitting with his slices. "He took out a gun and shoved it in my face and told me to open the register. He only wanted the big bills under the drawer, so I gave him the five fifties and a twenty."

"Son of a bitch," Little Joey said. He grabbed the baseball bat again and clomped to the front door. The pictures on the walls rattled with each heavy footfall.

"He's already gone," Vic said, as Little Joey stormed out onto the sidewalk and peered into the dark. On his way back inside, Little Joey grabbed a bent pizza crust off the ground and winged it into the nearest garbage can. Watching this, Vic wondered if Little Joey would suspect him of taking the money. Would he ask Vic to open his wallet, to empty his pockets? Or did Little Joey somehow already know about Vic's selfish cowardice?

Little Joey pushed Vic aside and opened the register. He checked under the drawer, did a quick count of the cash, and then picked up the cordless.

As Little Joey dialed his dad's home number, Vic asked him the question.

"Aren't you going to ask me if I took the money?"

Little Joey clamped the phone between his ear and shoulder and looked Vic up and down. He shook his head with a laugh and gave Vic a joking slap to the back of the head.

"Wiseass," he said, with brotherly affection.

VANLIFE

For the past two weeks I've been living out of my van. It's not a lifestyle for everyone, but at this juncture of my life, it was the best move for me. I mean, I'm twenty-two, soon to be twenty-three, so I can't be living with my parents anymore. With one kid in preschool and another one on the way, that's not how a grown-up adult is supposed to live his life. That's what my girlfriend Lauren always says, and you know what? I agree with her. She tends to be right about most things. And this was the perfect time to make the move, career-wise, because my boss Rooster just got arrested for selling cocaine and oxy out of the back of his BBQ joint where I work as a waiter, and that's not a situation I want my budding family to be associated with. So I took Lauren's advice and quit. Well, that's not entirely true. I didn't formally quit, since I have no way of contacting Rooster while he's being held in protective custody so he doesn't get killed by the Gulf Cartel for losing millions of dollars of their product, but since Rooster always paid me in cash and never kept any records of any kind, I don't think I have to tell him I can't be one of his waiters anymore if sometime in the future he gets out of prison and eludes the cartel death squads long enough to open a new BBQ joint that could somehow be profitable without accurate record keeping and no drugs. But as far-fetched as that sounds, Rooster is probably the one guy who could pull it off. He really is a great BBQ man. His dry rub recipe is incredible. It's got just the right mix of spicy, smoky, and sweet. Plus he's got all kinds of connections in the BBQ world and I assume he has a lot of money stashed away, so he could probably get a good price on a new custom smoker built by one of the pros. Then again, he might not have any money left. I don't know the truth either way because we were never that tight, he was just my boss after all, but he's a huge guy with a huge belly and a huge laugh and a huge appetite. Not just for BBQ ribs and sliced brisket and pulled pork and smoked sausage and jalapeño pineapple slaw and all that good stuff, but for everything really. Women, whiskey, blow, oxy, cars, guns, and exotic animals. So it's entirely possible he could have no money left at all. And that's fine, because Lauren said it's time for me to step up and to be a man and to stop being a chickenshit loser and to support my family by getting a real job that pays with a check instead of a handful of crumpled-up bills stuffed into a plastic baggie dusted with white powder. So I guess it's time to forget about Rooster. But that's pretty hard to do when you're unemployed and driving around all day looking for work in a 1996 maroon Dodge minivan with no air conditioning and three doors that don't lock. It's even harder to do when you're parked overnight in a Wal-Mart parking lot and a homeless guy clomps up beside your van and starts taking a dump right there on the pavement. It's this kind of a situation that can make a man envious of his former employer's BBQ glory and hedonistic lifestyle. It can also make a man so resentful of his current station in life that he bursts out of his 1996 maroon Dodge minivan and beats said homeless guy with his own filthy sneaker until said homeless guy's face looks like a smashed watermelon leaking juice onto the dusty pavement. That's another possibility. But it's not the only one. This same situation could also inspire a man to scramble back into the driver's seat of his 1996 maroon Dodge minivan and drive across town to Wendy's for a late-night spicy chicken sandwich. Or, there could be a third possibility that branches off from the second, where, after driving across town for a spicy chicken sandwich, the man could discover that his 1996 maroon Dodge minivan exceeds the height limit for the twenty-four-hour drive-thru lane at Wendy's, thereby forcing him to walk up to the drive-thru window on foot, which itself might result in him getting into an argument with the Wendy's drive-thru person. In this third possibility, the Wendy's drive-thru person would probably yell some very rude and impolite things at him due to the fact that he's on foot and not in a vehicle like all the other customers, but in the end, she'd most likely take his order of a spicy chicken sandwich because he's a paying customer with money, just like everyone else, the only difference being some unfortunate reddish stains on his clothes and his lack of a vehicle that fits in the drive-thru lane. But these are just possibilities. And Lauren doesn't need to know about every possibility that can arise from my new lifestyle, no matter how adventurous and exciting it may be. Between our son, her folks, and the coming baby, she's got enough on her plate as it is.

OTHERWORLD

Three weeks after Ron turned sixty, his doctor told him to lose fifty pounds.

"Your blood pressure is through the roof, Ron," the doctor said, "and your cholesterol is none too pretty."

Later that evening, when Ron called his son Cliff and told him about what the doctor had said, Cliff suggested he make some videos about his weight loss journey and put them on the internet.

"That way, other people will know you're trying to lose weight, and you won't be able to quit so easily," Cliff said. From the time on the clock, Ron knew Cliff was biking home from work right now, and his son's voice, traveling from San Francisco to New York in less than a second, sounded strange and altered, as if it had passed through another dimension in order to get here. "Your viewers will hold you accountable and cheer you on at the same time. And I think that'll be good for you, you know, with Mom gone."

Hearing this, Ron started to tell his son how unnatural the idea of a diet felt to him, of how, as the youngest of seven brothers, the dinner table had been a battlefield when he was growing up, and that if he didn't eat as much as he could as fast as he could, there wouldn't have been anything left on his plate the next time he looked down. But before Ron could finish saying this, his son cut him off.

"I know, Dad, I know," Cliff said, a car horn blaring on his end. "You've told me about your dinnertime war stories a thousand times. I just hope you'll use some of that tenacity to get healthy this time. Because it's important. Me and Brandon are worried about you, living in that big house all by yourself."

Hearing the genuine concern in his son's voice, Ron realized he owed it to his boy to at least try the idea. So he bought a webcam, hooked it up to his computer, and searched the internet for instructions on how to set up a YouTube channel.

The first few videos didn't get many views. Maybe twenty or so per video. But after a while some more people started watching. That part wasn't too hard. The real challenge was the diet itself. Because with Connie gone, Ron could eat whatever he wanted, whenever he wanted to. And despite what Cliff had said, there was nothing Ron's viewers could do to stop him each time he lumbered into the kitchen to make his fourth peanut butter and jelly sandwich of the night.

ს———ი

A few weeks later, someone in the comments of one of Ron's videos told him about something called the grapefruit diet. Since Ron had gained weight in the past few weeks instead of losing, he decided to look into the grapefruit thing. After all, Cliff and Brandon would be flying in for Christmas next month, and if he still looked like this when his son walked through the door, Cliff would know in an instant that he'd skipped out on the diet.

Ron searched the internet for the grapefruit diet. According to the article he found, the grapefruit diet allowed the dieter to eat and drink as much as he wanted, whenever he wanted to, as long as it was grapefruit. Fresh grapefruit, frozen grapefruit, sliced, diced, juiced, anything. He liked the sound of that. Since his wife had been taken from him twenty years too early, he'd had it with removing things from his life. So a diet that allowed him to eat as much as he wanted, whenever he wanted to, sounded like a gift from the gods.

He started the grapefruit diet the next morning.

꜀— —꜀

It was hell.

Four days into the grapefruit diet, Ron stopped eating. He couldn't take it anymore. Dying of starvation would've been less painful than taking another stinging bite of that burning pink demon flesh.

For the next three days he didn't eat at all. This wasn't too difficult during work hours at the bank, but once he got home each night, the minutes passed with the speed of a glacier carving through a continent. To survive the long evenings alone, he took to the internet and read about his favorite subject: mythology. Greek, Roman, Norse, and Celtic. Ever since he was a kid, he had loved the stories of the squabbling gods, the magical creatures, and the honorable heroes. At the time these stories had helped him feel better about his own turbulent home life, because if the most powerful beings in the universe acted this way, violently punishing their children, dishonoring their families, and betraying their brothers and sisters, then it wasn't as bad when everyone in his own family did those same things to each other. Though he hadn't talked to any of his brothers in over twenty years, he realized that these stories were the only reason he had stayed in contact with them for as long as he had.

∽— —∾

When Ron woke up the next morning, his fourth consecutive day of not eating, he found a giant in his bedroom. The giant stood nearly eight feet tall, and he wore a long red robe of rough, thick fabric. A beard the color of wet earth clung to the giant's chin, but the rest of his face lay hidden behind the heavy cloth of his red hood. In addition to this, Ron saw a bubbling stone cauldron floating just above the floor near the giant's feet. From the cauldron rose the delicious smells of roasted pork, baked potatoes, and freshly churned butter.

Before Ron could react to this sight, the giant started speaking. He introduced himself as the Dagda, one of the gods Ron knew from the stories of Celtic mythology. Soon Ron realized the giant was probably just a hallucination of his calorie-deprived brain, so he climbed out of bed, slipped past the rambling Dagda, and went into the kitchen for a well-deserved breakfast.

When he got there he found nothing in the fridge but grapefruits. Following this he went back into his room and started to get dressed to go out. It was only a few minutes after nine on Sunday morning, but he knew the CVS just outside the neighborhood would be open, and that was good enough for him.

While Ron sat on the edge of his bed and got dressed, the Dagda kept talking. He talked about the race of gods he ruled over, the *Tuatha Dé Danann*; his cauldron of plenty that never runs dry, the *Coire Ansic*; and how he traveled to this small town in upstate New York to lend his aid to the starving Ron, who had not eaten in three days. Then he pointed at the cauldron at his feet and offered Ron all the roasted pork, baked potatoes, and freshly churned butter he could eat.

As hard as it was to refuse the offer, Ron politely declined and walked to the front door. He figured it was a bad idea to take food from a hooded giant who had mysteriously appeared in his bedroom overnight.

Outside, the sharp November air gnawed at the end of Ron's nose, the tips of his thick fingers.

For a moment Ron considered climbing into his silver Honda and driving to the CVS, but then he turned toward the end of the driveway and decided to walk. If his mind was messed up enough to be seeing Celtic gods, then it was probably not a good idea to be driving anywhere.

It was a cold, quiet morning. A milky fog floated in the air, and gravel crunched softly underfoot. To Ron's right the Dagda hovered just above the ground, his cauldron of plenty swaying lightly in the fog.

As they walked down the hill to the end of the neighborhood, the Dagda spoke about his cauldron of plenty. He talked about how its ladle was large enough to hold two men, about how no human had ever walked away from it unsatisfied. After this he looked down at Ron and once again offered an endless feast of roasted pork, baked potatoes, and freshly churned butter. When Ron declined, the Dagda offered the feast a third time, and then described the food on offer. In great detail he talked about the tenderness of the pork, the heartiness of the potatoes, and the creamy fat of the butter. But as delicious as everything sounded, Ron ignored the bearded god and kept walking.

For the next few minutes Ron thought about his departed wife Connie, his concerned son Cliff, and the empty house waiting for him at the top of the hill. He tried to think of a way he could survive in that house by himself for the next twenty years, but everything he imagined involved him burying his loneliness under a mountain of unhealthy food. And as his doctor had made clear last month, that was no longer an option.

Minutes later the Dagda stopped talking and rested his massive hands on Ron's shoulders. In a booming voice he announced that Ron had passed the supreme test of courage and could now enter *Tír na nÓg*, the Celtic otherworld of eternal youth, joy, health, and plenty. From here the Dagda explained that his offers of endless feasts had been a test to challenge the courage and resolve of the starving Ron, and by refusing all three of these offers, Ron had proved his worthiness. Pointing at a wall of fog at the end of the street, the Dagda told Ron to walk in that direction.

"There you will meet a beautiful woman with golden hair," the Dagda said. "She will offer you a silver apple branch. Take the branch, and she will lead you to *Tír na nÓg*."

Since the place the Dagda had pointed at was the direction he was already going, Ron followed the Dagda's instructions and walked through the fog.

Moments later, Ron stepped through the front door of the CVS. A skinny high school boy with frizzy blond hair stood in one of the aisles, stocking candy bars on an endcap. When he sensed Ron staring at him, he turned around and held out a 3 Musketeers candy bar. The silver wrapper gleamed in the fluorescent light.

"Need one of these?" the boy said.

"I think I'll take two, just in case," Ron said.

⌒﹏⌒

Thirty minutes later, with two silver candy wrappers balled in his pocket, Ron stepped into his house and closed the door behind him. Now that he was finally alone again, he walked into the kitchen, grabbed a pen and paper, and called his son Cliff. By the second ring Ron realized it was not yet seven a.m. on the west coast, but he stayed on the line anyway. This call was too important. He didn't want to hang up and let this feeling slip away.

Cliff picked up on the fourth ring.

"Sorry to call you so early, son, but I've had a weird morning."

"What happened? Is everything okay?" Cliff said, his voice breathless and urgent with concern.

"Everything's fine, I'll tell you about it later, but listen. Can you give me an idea of what I *should* be eating in order to get healthy? Because they're crazy, all these people in the comments of my videos. Everything they say is crazy, and I don't even know where to start."

THANK YOU, MADAME CLARA

Hey Madame Clara, it's so great to talk to you again! I'm not sure if you remember me, but I'm Lightning the Interdimensional Cheetah, and a few weeks ago I called you because I was really scared to reveal my fursona to my parents for the first time, and you were the one who gave me the confidence to—yeah, exactly! Wow, I didn't think you'd remember me with all the people you—haha, that's true, I'm the only interdimensional cheetah *I've* ever met too, and ... I know, I got so sad when I saw on the website that your psychic hotline is going out of business after so many ... exactly! That's what I was just going to say, I think *everyone* should be coming to you for advice, considering how messed up the world is these days, with all the, the ... well you know, just everything that's been happening, I don't really pay attention to the news unless it has to do with anime or cartoons or a new furry convention, but anyway, I just wanted to call in one last time and thank you for your amazing vision and the great advice you gave me that day, because it literally changed my life ... well, things didn't work out exactly the way you said they would, because my parents were actually pretty pissed when I finally revealed my fursona to them, but ...

well I mean I did it exactly how you told me to, I wore my fursuit when I told them that I'm Lightning the Interdimensional Cheetah and that I can run one-tenth the speed of light, but before I could say anything else, my dad got really angry and started yelling curse words while my mom just sat on the couch and cried, so that was, that was pretty different from how it went in your dream, but that was actually for the best, because when they tried to force me to find a therapist the next day, I just searched the internet for the nearest furry convention, and it turned out that there was going to be a pretty big one in this place upstate called Barrier that's like two hours from where I live in Topine, so I told my parents that I found a great therapist and that it would cost two hundred dollars for the first two sessions, and then while they were at work a few days later, I packed my fursuit and some snacks and other clothes into my car, and I took the two hundred dollars they gave me, and I started the drive up to the Holiday Inn in Barrier where the convention was going to be and—what's that? Yeah, no, I left them a note to tell them I was okay . . . ummmm, I actually don't remember what I wrote on the note, but that doesn't matter because I haven't even gotten to the best part yet which is . . . no, no I haven't talked to them since then because I've had my cell phone turned off, and I've been using one of those prepaid burner phones they sell at Best Buy for like—yes, yes, *okay*, for fuck's sake, I'll call them soon, Christ almighty, you sound exactly like my mom . . . yeah I know they're probably worried sick, but to be honest, if they had taken two goddamn seconds to try to understand me and accept me for who I really—Oh! That reminds me! I just remembered why I called! I'm in love! Yeah! It was at the Furrycon here in Barrier that I met her, and I swear, Madame Clara, you should've seen her, she—well I still don't know her real name, and I haven't seen any part of her human body since we both have pretty bad social anxiety and we're nowhere near the yiff stage yet, but— what's that? oh yiff is just uh . . . it's like, uh . . . sexy stuff, you know, sexy-time stuff, and—yeah, we haven't quite gotten there yet, but I—no, all I know is her fursona, Pringles the Arctic Fox, and . . . yeah it is, she named her after her favorite chips, which are my favorite chips too! Isn't that so crazy? Haha well of course *you* don't think so because you already knew what was going to happen the whole time, but I'm glad *I* finally understand what you meant when you told me that great minds think—yeah, coming! That's Pringles at the door right now. Our hotel rooms are right on the same floor, how crazy is that? I think it's fate, but I'm sure you saw that coming, too. Anyway, got to go. Be right there, Pringy!

CICADAS

It was just before eight on a hot Tuesday in July and I was driving to work past the farms and fields on Grove. I felt like shit like always and I couldn't deal with customers and coupons today, so I pulled onto the side of the road in front of an old abandoned barn squatting beside an eighty-foot oak standing near a beautiful rolling field cleaved by a collapsing wooden fence. With gold sunlight warming my face, I walked behind the barn and called Kyoko on her cell. For an hour we sat in the prickly grass and listened to the cicadas buzzing in the heat. Everything was calm. The world was peaceful. And for the first time in months, I was happy. But then the sky turned white and the cicadas went silent and glittering gray snow started falling from the sky. Without a word, K squeezed my hand and let me know it was time to leave. As we jogged back to our cars, I watched the gray snowflakes slicing through the still air, glinting in the milky light, spinning like tiny sawblades.

STATUES

When the earth shook beneath us and the black smoke churned into the sky, me and Kyoko emptied the food from the fridge and closed ourselves off in the basement. Looking up at the greasy window near the ceiling, we pressed our phones to the grimy glass and filmed our neighbors as they streamed into the street in a daze. Their eyes were glued to their phones; their faces were blank and distracted; their fingers flicked endlessly to the sky. When the pyroclastic flow mummified us moments later, these are the statues we became.

CANVAS

Me and Kyoko went on a hike in the woods out by Kentor Mountain. Spears of gold light fell through the trees as jewels of warm sweat rolled down our faces. Around noon we came upon a lush clearing in which prairie grass, wood lily, and corn mint bloomed in orange and green. At the edge of the clearing, we found an old man painting the scene before us. On his canvas, the clearing was a wasteland of roaring orange flame and black smoke billowing into the sky. In the center of the painting, the old man's charred corpse lay on the ground in front of his burning canvas. Me and K looked at the painting and then each other. She spoke first.

"Is that you in the middle of the painting?"

"Yes," the old man said, without taking his eyes off the canvas.

"But why would you paint something like that?" K said.

"This is what happens next," the old man said. "It's not for me to decide."

I looked at the lower third of the canvas, which remained unfinished.

"Are we going to appear in the painting?" I said.

The old man croaked a dry laugh and stuck a cigarette between his cracked lips. He lit the cigarette with a match and dropped the burning match into the grass and went on painting.

K uncapped her water bottle and doused the match with a splash of water. Then she picked up the blackened match and dropped it in her bottle.

"That's incredibly irresponsible," she said.

The old man croaked another froggy laugh and sucked at his cigarette like a straw and scraped at his canvas with a painter's knife. No one spoke for a time. After another minute of quiet, me and K clomped away down the trail.

When we returned hours later, the old man was gone. His finished painting lay face-up in the grass beside the trail, but this time we looked the other way: at red oaks and sugar maples and winged elms, at tiny insects flying through slants of light.

THE BLUE LIGHT

I woke up five minutes before my alarm went off. The glowing screen of my phone read ten a.m., but the coal-black sky suggested midnight. By noon it was even darker. The darkness had become aggressive, swallowing every bit of light in the house. Me and Kyoko tried calling our friends, our families, and our neighbors, but nothing worked. Our phones had become bricks of dead plastic. So we slipped them from our pockets and dropped them on the floor. Then we interlocked our fingers and stumbled to the front door.

Outside, we saw a dot of blue light in the distance. We walked toward it. Hours later we crunched across an abandoned parking lot that seemed to stretch on forever. In the center of the lot stood a single steel streetlight with a glowing blue sodium lamp. Though the dark had only been here for a day, the light burned our eyes worse than the sun. We didn't care. We stared at it anyway.

When we stepped into the cone of light, someone emerged from the darkness beside us. We couldn't see who it was. Our eyes didn't work right anymore. It didn't matter. Kyoko and I turned to the stranger.

Look, we said, pointing up at the blue bulb buzzing in the dark.

Look.

DINNER DATE

Since the first day of seventh grade, Aaron had been a runner. He loved the freedom of the winding roads, the slice of the cool wind, and the rhythm of his clopping shoes.

Years later, when his high school health teacher talked about the dangers of heart disease, the ravages of diabetes, and the importance of exercise, Aaron smiled to himself and looked out the window. Thanks to his love for running, he knew his health would never be a problem, so he stopped listening and pressed two fingers to his wrist. He liked to count his pulse to see how low he could get it to go.

In college, while standing at the start of the New York City Marathon, the icy November air knifing through his moisture-wicking running clothes, Aaron met a girl from Long Island named Libby. By the time Aaron crossed the upper level of the Verrazzano Bridge, he and Libby were already good friends.

After college Aaron and Libby moved back to Aaron's hometown of Topine, NY. There they started working as teachers at Aaron's old high school. Each fall Aaron coached the boys cross country team, and Libby coached the girls.

Years later, on what was supposed to be the first day of his fourteenth season as coach of the Topine High School

Boys Cross Country team, Aaron stayed home with the flu. To cover for her husband, Libby called the school and told them that she would be coaching both the boys and the girls cross country teams for the next week.

⌒⸻⌒

Sometime before noon, Aaron climbed out of bed and went into the kitchen for a banana. An instant later he found himself facedown on the floor in the hallway, his lips slicked with blood, his left cheek bruised and aching. For the first few moments after waking up, he didn't know who he was, where he was, or what the universe was. Soon this information came back to him, so he stood up and went into the bathroom to clean himself up. When he looked in the mirror, he found a horseshoe-shaped bite mark on his tongue. The bite mark was bright red and leaking blood. Seeing this he called Libby and told her to meet him at the hospital.

After various blood tests and an MRI, the doctors informed Aaron that he'd had a seizure caused by a tumor in his brain. But since the tumor was tightly wrapped around his brain stem, it was impossible to operate. They gave him six to twelve months to live.

⌒⸻⌒

Following his recovery from the flu, Aaron tried to go back to work to get his mind off the tumor. He only lasted a week. He was terribly afraid of dying, and he had never been a good actor.

On the following Monday, while Libby was at school for her final week of work before taking a leave of absence to care for her husband, Aaron sat at the kitchen table and tried to imagine what it would be like to be dead. He saw himself falling through infinite blackness, his body emptied of love and passion and sport and friendship.

An hour later he came to a conclusion. The blackness he could handle. The emptiness he could not.

So he went around the house and gathered all the things he could not let go of. These included his favorite pair of running shoes, the bronze medal from his first middle school race, some glossy photos from his and Libby's second marathon, and his Coach of the Year plaque from when his boys won the state championship.

Aaron laid these things on the bed and opened a black garbage bag from the kitchen. For the next few minutes he looked at the items and thought about what they meant to him. All the emotions they evoked, all the memories they brought to the surface. Once he had done this with each item, he tried to put them in the bag, but he couldn't do it. They were everything he'd ever been, and without them he would be empty forever. So he picked up his Coach of the Year plaque and smacked himself in the forehead with it. Not hard. Just hard enough to force himself to accept the reality of his situation. But this first little hit didn't do anything, so he hit himself again, this time a little harder. Still nothing. The next few minutes saw more hits: first nose, then chin, then cheekbone. Soon he grew tired of this game, so he bashed the plaque against his jaw and felt something break. His entire head roared with pulsing pain. Despite this, he still felt empty and afraid. To rid himself of these feelings, he grabbed the baseball bat beside his bed, smashed his plaque in half, and jammed the splintered wood down his throat. Then he grabbed his running shoes and choked those down as well, one right after the other. Next came the photos of him and Libby from their second marathon, and the bronze medal from his first middle school race. All of it down the hatch.

None of it helped. He still felt empty, alone, and terrified. Then, as he sat on the floor and thought about where he had gone wrong, he finally realized his mistake. All these objects were just *symbols* of what he loved, not the real thing. If he wanted true peace, he'd need the genuine article.

For the next few hours, Aaron cleaned himself up and started preparing a special dinner in anticipation of Libby's return. His broken jaw still hung loose and limp beneath his face, but that didn't matter now. He had no more use for words. All that mattered was dinner. Dinner was going to be a very special meal tonight, the most special one he had ever shared with his wife, and he wanted everything to be perfect.

WHAT REMAINED
AFTER THE EXPLOSION

Following the third explosion on the third island in three years, Dunbar and Pike went alone to assess the damage. There they found a flooded crater of silt and powdered glass in the place where their nitroglycerin processing plant used to be. Walking the rim of the crater, Dunbar found the partially melted heel of a leather workboot sticking up out of the ground. He crouched above the boot and waved Pike over for a look.

"Christ," Pike said.

"I know," Dunbar said.

The earth around the boot started to move. Dunbar and Pike jumped backward in surprise. A naked man erupted through the glittering crust of silt and powdered glass. Uninjured, the man's skin glowed as pink and fresh as an infant emerging from a bathtub.

The man fished the workboot out of the ground and poured the silt from the interior of the boot. He slid the filthy boot onto his foot and tugged at the blackened tongue. Dunbar and Pike gaped in disbelief as the man laced up his boot and clumped into the center of the crater. Before the two industrialists could say another word the man was gone, slipping soundlessly beneath the mirrored surface of the water.

THE PEOPLE IN THE WALLS

Me and Sis waded the flooded hallways of the abandoned building, searching for edible food and clean water. Our bellies hung empty and distended beneath our chins; our tongues lay huge and dry and cracked inside our mouths.

As we clomped in slow motion down a long corridor, the water scudding swiftly past our waists, we watched small, flat-bodied people wage war with each other inside the walls. Wearing ancient clothes or few clothes or no clothes at all, they stabbed and slashed and burned many others of their kind, mostly men, but some women and children and animals too. Me and Sis kept walking. We didn't say a word. We had seen so much of that already.

Farther down the corridor we discovered a vast, complex city the flat-bodied people had built inside the walls. Gridded streets of stone lined with granite obelisks yawned along the ceiling above our heads. A magnificent temple of painted marble unfurled along the floor beneath our feet. A hamlet of mudbrick huts capped with roofs of thatched straw crowded into the narrow corner where wall met ceiling. As we continued on, we noticed that the two-dimensional city was empty of all life, and its streets were stained brown with old blood.

When me and Sis reached the end of the corridor, the walls lay bare; the storage rooms sat empty; the flat-bodied people were gone without a trace. Sis drew a long, slow breath and looked at me. We turned around and began the trudge back home.

MIRRORS AND MORE MIRRORS

Toby wakes up for work at 7:08 and trudges into the bathroom to pee. Once finished, he dodges the scale for the nineteenth day in a row and looks in the mirror. In his bathroom there are mirrors on two walls, in front and behind, so each time he gathers the courage to look at himself he sees a corridor of clones retreating off into infinity. But a single look this morning makes him feel like steamrolled shit, so to take his mind off his bloated, disgusting body, he leans toward the mirror and examines a coarse black hair spiking out of his right nostril. All his clones do the same thing, all except one about ten universes back. The rogue clone watches with disgust as Toby stands inches from the mirror, looking up his nose. Then the rogue clone bends down, picks up a bucket of fried chicken, and crunches into a drumstick. As Toby watches him chomp away, his lips slicked with grease, fat beads of sweat start scudding down Toby's forehead. A cold tingle spreads to the ends of Toby's fingers. A sharp pain shoots through his left arm. His heart thuds like a boulder rolling down a hill. Gasping for breath, Toby watches as his clones crumple to the floor, dead, until only him and the rogue clone are still standing. The rogue clone stares at Toby for a long time, sucking shining strips of dark meat off the bone of his drumstick. The rogue clone drops the bone to the floor of his universe, where it clinks against something hard and metal. Then he reaches into the bucket and picks up another drumstick. Toby grasps the edge of the sink with both hands and tries to take a deep breath, but he hardly gets any air. The rogue clone mouths something and gestures at Toby's naked body with the fat end of his drumstick. Toby can't make out the words, but he nods anyway.

Just before his legs buckle beneath him, Toby lowers himself to the floor and stares up at the ceiling. There he sees a silky gray spider web clinging to the grille of the overhead ventilation fan. Toby slurps a shallow, trembling breath. A few moments later, a frighteningly large yellow-and-black spider slowly descends from the network of webs threaded between the tines of the grille. Toby tries to swat it away, but he doesn't have the strength to lift his arms. Just before the spider touches down, Toby stretches his neck to the side and glances in the mirror above the sink. There he sees the rogue clone standing in the universe right next to his own, going to town on a foot-long Philly cheesesteak. Toby's stomach grumbles angrily as it fills with more junk food. The spider lands on the front of Toby's shoulder. Finally understanding the fractured logic of his situation, Toby leans his head back and offers his neck to the spider. A hot, sharp sting sears the flesh just below his chin. Tongues of cold fire engulf his neck, his head, his shoulders, his chest. Toby looks in the mirror and waits for the rogue clone to claw at his throat. To choke on his cheesesteak. For his face to turn purple and swell up like a balloon. But the rogue clone takes another huge bite of his cheesesteak and points at Toby's neck. Toby tries to lower his head, but he can't. A hard, painful blister the size of a lemon is in the way. Toby glances in the mirror again. The rogue clone shrugs and mashes the remaining stump of his cheesesteak into his mouth. He walks away. A heavy metal door opens and then clangs shut. A hairline fracture sprouts in the center of the mirror. Toby closes his eyes and tries to take a breath. Jewels of milky sweat pool on the cold tile floor.

FRIDAY NIGHT
AT THE PINE VALLEY MALL

On Friday night, me and Kyoko drive out to the Pine Valley Mall. The mall shut down six years ago, but we still go every weekend. It's something of a tradition of ours. It's where we first met back in the nineties, standing in line at Wendy's in the food court. At the time I never knew what to say to girls, so without thinking, I forced myself to ask her the first thing that came into my mind: *what are you going to order?* Turning her head a little bit to the side, just enough to glance at me from the corners of her glinting amber eyes, she said, *two spicy chicken sandwiches.* Then she winked and turned back around. I don't know why she winked or what that gesture meant, but it was the coolest thing I'd ever seen anybody do. I fell for her right there.

Her old words replay in my head as we park in the mall's abandoned parking lot and slip past the thick chain and reinforced steel padlock sealing off the entrance to what used to be JCPenny. After I clamber up a gutter pipe hidden behind the skeleton of a dead hedge, I lay on my stomach on the roof and reach down for Kyoko's bulky backpack. She tosses it up to me; my arm aches and quivers as I pull it up; I rest the backpack on the roof and rub the burn from my shoulder. Then I reach down and hold out my hand to help her up. She shoots me a look of amused annoyance and whispers a single word.

Please.

I nod, pull back my hand, and get out of her way. In seven seconds she's up on the roof beside me, huffing from the effort of the climb.

Five minutes later I jump down through a broken skylight and into the hollow corpse of an old Sam Goody music shop. My favorite store back in high school. A sharp sting buzzes through my knees upon impact, but thankfully, whoever used to come here before us dragged an old water-stained mattress beneath the skylight to cushion the fall. Standing under the skylight, I open my arms and wait for Kyoko to carefully drop her backpack. Once that's safe with me, I tell her to jump down. I tell her I'll catch her. I remind her I never miss. This time she doesn't argue. After counting down from three, she drops into my arms. Her heel bangs hard into my shoulder and sends a hot spike of pain darting down my side, but she grins at me and lets out a giddy little giggle, so I swallow a pained groan and place her on her feet.

Out in the dark hallway, Kyoko clicks on her flashlight and grabs hold of my hand. She scans the heavy gloom to make sure we're alone. She looks at me and nods.

Come on, she says, in a swishing whisper.

Breaking into a run, Kyoko pulls me toward the expanse of filthy tile that used to be the food court. Our footsteps click on the hard floors; our huffing breath echoes through the dead mall; we dodge puddles of scummy water browning the tile before us. Following the swinging cylinder of sharp blue light coughed out by

Kyoko's LED flashlight, we reach the food court in two minutes. Hugging the wall to our left, we slow to a leisurely walk and admire the line of thirty or forty paintings hanging on the wall. Each painting is a still life of a spicy chicken sandwich from Wendy's. As we progress farther along the wall, we watch in delight as the paintings grow more expert and realistic, before taking a sudden turn into strangeness and surrealism. Stopping at each painting and furrowing our brows in a parody of haughty, pretentious, all-too-serious art collectors, we make silly comments to each other about the paintings.

When we reach the end of the line of paintings, Kyoko kneels down and unzips her backpack. She hands me a hammer, two nails, and two pieces of sturdy twine. Then she removes her two most recent artworks. The first is a still life of the spicy chicken sandwich seen in ads, the version with the giant, crispy, perfectly cut slab of chicken housed within an artistically crafted bun. The second is a crude pencil drawing of the high school versions of us fucking between the misshapen, deflated bun you get in the real-life version of the sandwich.

I pick up the two artworks, fasten a piece of twine to the back of each canvas, and hammer the two nails into the next vacant spots on the wall. Then I move aside and watch as Kyoko hangs up her newest works. Taking a few steps back, she holds up her phone and snaps a few pictures of the newest additions to her gallery. She slips her phone back into her pocket and looks at me. A wide grin slices across her face. She points at the pencil-line drawing of us fucking between the buns of the sad-sack spicy chicken sandwich.

"I think this one is my favorite," she says, her grin widening.

"It's your masterpiece," I say, throwing my arm around her shoulders and nodding in agreement.

THANKSGIVING EVE

Skip went out to the bars in town to see people for the first time since getting struck by lightning. In the five months since the strike, lingering anxiety had kept him trapped inside his house, afraid of the empty sky; but he knew he would never move on with his life unless he faced his fear, so he forced himself to text his old best friend from high school, Jem, and make plans to go out. It was the night before Thanksgiving, and everyone from high school was back home for the holiday.

Due to his lightning injuries (headaches, dizziness, brain fog, nerve damage in his right arm), Skip could no longer drive; so he bummed a ride off his dad and stepped through the front door of 49's Pub a little after ten p.m. Unsurprisingly, the place was packed. Clusters of bearded guys with shining, styled hair and analog watches of brushed steel joked loudly near flat-screen TVs affixed to the walls. Mixed groups of men and women in their thirties sat at square tables and chatted over half-empty glasses and froth-stitched pitchers of beer. One-time acquaintances and people he had known but never met passed by with less hair, plumper faces, unfamiliar glasses, new piercings, fresh tattoos, glittering wedding rings, and grinning partners from other states.

The plan had been for him to meet Jem at the end of the bar at ten-thirty, but he could see that in this crowd that would be impossible. So he camped out by the window and kept an eye on the front door. Soon after getting there, he heard a voice yell his name.

"Hold up, is that Skip?" the voice, a guy's, a little slurred, slightly familiar, bellowed from somewhere on the left.

At this sound Skip turned and saw one of his freshman year lunch buddies pushing through the crowd toward him, but no matter how hard he tried, he couldn't remember the guy's name, or anything else about him.

"Dude!" the guy said, stepping up next to Skip. He wore a fur-lined aviator jacket over a loud Hawaiian button-up and black jeans. Cinched loosely around his waist and drooping low on his left hip was a sky blue fanny pack.

"Hey man," Skip said, holding his hand out for a handshake.

"You died!" the guy said, his left hand palming his shaved head in disbelief, his right hovering at his side with an unlit cigarette clamped between his pointer and middle finger.

"Well, technically, but I've been back for a while," Skip said with a chuckle, trying to make a joke out of this thing that had not left his mind for the past five months.

"Hold up, hold up," the guy said, his expression suddenly turning serious. The sour plume of booze- and tobacco-drenched breath billowing from his mouth made Skip's eyes water, his head ache. "You need to tell me the truth right now. Did you or did you not experience the jewel-like treasure of your life expiring from this mortal coil of being that we call planet Earth? I need an answer on this."

"Yeah, I mean, that's what the guy who saved me said had happened, but I don't really have any memory of it myself," Skip said, feeling his heartbeat quicken at having to think about that day again. It was true that he had no memory of being struck under a blue sky, or of his heart stopping for ninety seconds, or of his life being saved by an off-duty EMT who happened to be walking his dog two hundred feet away, but his memory of that June day wasn't completely empty. He could still remember those awful things he had felt moments after waking up in the grass: the suffocating confusion that crashed over him all at once, like a wall of water; the raw fear so heavy it had been difficult to breathe; the uncontrollable trembling of his first panic attack.

But that day was the last thing he wanted to be thinking about right now, so he shook his head and shrugged. "It was just an instant for me. One second I was jogging through the park, warming down from my run, and the next I was waking up on the ground with a random guy doing CPR on me."

Skip's friend frowned and studied Skip's expression closely for another few seconds.

"I understand. You're not comfortable enough yet to talk about what really happened. That makes sense. But the expression on your face right now tells me you experienced something transcendent and indescribable. I can see it in your eyes."

Hearing these words, a needle of cold adrenaline forked up the side of Skip's neck. In an instant he felt his heart thudding, his fingers twitching.

"It's really not anything like that, I just—" Skip started to say, but before he could finish his sentence, a stocky guy with long black hair and a thick mustache like a paintbrush crashed into him from behind, and sent the room spinning. Following this the mustache guy turned around, grabbed Skip's shoulders, and started brushing imaginary dirt from them.

Skip shook hands with the mustache guy to make him go away. But even after he was gone, Skip still felt dizzy and anxious from the shove, so he started for the bathroom to calm himself down. Before he could get away, his old lunch buddy threw an arm around his shoulder and started walking him toward the smokers' deck.

"I was just thinking the same thing. I feel like I need a smoke every time I'm forced to interact with the Cro-Magnons that live in this town these days," his friend said, shouting into his ear. Feeling the soft, lumpy jab of his friend's fanny pack pressing into his side, Skip was pretty sure the man was carrying drugs in there. "But more importantly, I've got a very interesting question for you. Step into my office. This is something you need to hear."

Skip searched his rattled brain for an excuse to leave, but a few seconds of hard thinking turned up nothing. It was true that he wasn't yet ready to face his fear and stroll outside under the dangerous sky, but after hearing his friend bellow across the room without a care a few minutes ago, Skip knew he wouldn't be able to get away without his friend creating another boisterous scene like the one the mustache guy had just caused. And if that happened, Skip ran the risk of being thrown out of the pub for good. So, after working through the calculus of anxiety inside his head, Skip took a deep breath, gathered what courage he could, and followed his friend through the side door.

Out on the deck, Skip felt a cool wave of relief when he saw that the entire area was roofed by a long, canvas awning. In the back of his mind he knew that a quarter-inch-thick piece of canvas offered no protection whatsoever from the sizzling fury of a stray bolt of lightning, but the illusion of safety was convincing enough to temporarily ease his anxiety.

From here Skip and his friend squeezed through a murmuring crowd of more than forty shivering smokers. The temperature had dropped significantly in the time since Skip's short, frantic jog from his dad's idling car to the front door of the pub, and now the cold gnawed at the end of his nose, the lobes of his ears, and the tips of his fingers on his left hand. Soon his friend found an open spot near the edge of the deck and here he settled his back against the metal railing overlooking Miller's Creek.

"So Skip," Skip's lunch buddy said, leaning his head back and exhaling a plume of gray smoke, "are you familiar with a phenomenon called quantum immortality?"

"I was actually about to go back to school for that stuff before I got struck, but I haven't touched any of it since then. I don't think I could tell you a single thing about it now."

"You serious?"

"Yeah. I had always loved science and math when I was a kid, and then about a year ago I got back into it. I was going to go back to school up at Topine CC this fall, and then transfer to a four-year school after that. Had registered for classes and everything," Skip said, staring into the crowd. "But you know. Didn't work out."

"That sucks. Sorry to hear it, friend. But I'm glad you told me that, because from what you just said, and from what I've heard about your experience, I believe you're living proof that quantum immortality is real."

Lacking the energy to try to steer the conversation in another direction, Skip listened as his friend told him about quantum immortality.

"Back in the sixties there was a scientist named Hugh Everett who came up with a theory called the Many Worlds Interpretation of quantum physics. This theory states that every possible outcome of every event actually happens, just in different universes . . ."

Just then Skip felt his phone vibrate in his pocket. As his friend continued on with his monologue, Skip checked the text. It was from Jem.

Hey man, I'm running a little late, sorry bout that. Just walking up to 49's now. See you in a few.

Using the railing to steady his shaky right hand, Skip responded with a quick, *no worries, I'll meet you inside.*

". . . and if *that's* the case, which, based on Everett's thought experiment, I believe it is, that would mean that your current consciousness has transcended at least one, but possibly *multiple* other universes in order to be here with me in this continuum—" Skip's friend said, just before Skip rapped him on the shoulder and interrupted his lecture.

"That sounds pretty crazy man, but I got to go, I'm meeting someone inside," Skip said. From here he wormed through the crowd toward the door back into the pub.

Skip stepped back inside. Moments later a flash of movement near the back wall caught his eye. There he saw Jem sitting alone in one of the corner booths. Skip had no idea how anyone could walk into the busiest bar in town on the busiest night of the year and snag a corner booth without a minute of waiting, but apparently Jem was the one person who could do just that. Ever since they'd been friends, Jem had always managed to be in the right place at the right time. If it had been Jem running through the park on that June day, Skip speculated with jealousy, the lightning probably would've forked around his shoulders and struck the EMT instead.

Skip walked up to Jem's booth. Ten feet out he felt a wide smile slice across his face. He couldn't believe how *adult* Jem looked. Gone was his old lazy-guy uniform of grimy gray sweatshirt, baggy khakis, and chunky, grass-stained running shoes. In its place was a sophisticated ensemble consisting of a sleek black blazer, stonewashed designer jeans, and shining, black leather oxfords. And where baby-fat roundness and a slight double chin had once rendered his face childlike and immature, a sharp, square jaw and a pair of high cheekbones now aged him up to manhood. In the seven years since they had last seen each other before going off to college, it seemed that Jem had transformed himself into a full-blown adult.

To distract from his idiot grin, Skip held his arms out at his sides and gestured at the empty booth.

"Only you. Only you could walk in on Thanksgiving eve and just slide right into a booth like it's nothing. Must be nice."

Jem stood up to meet Skip and pulled him into a hearty hug complete with a series of firm thumps on the back.

"I know, lucky break right? I caught a group of my brother's friends just as they were heading out, and they let me nab it. But anyway, it's great to see you man, how are you? I heard about all the crazy shit that happened to you. Are you okay? Tell me what's going on," Jem said, releasing the hug and sliding back into the booth.

Skip sat down across from him and rested his hands on the table, but for some reason, he couldn't meet Jem's eyes.

"Yeah, it's great to see you too, you look so—you're like the GQ Man, seriously, you're looking sharp."

"Thank you, thank you," Jem said with a jokey bow. "So what's going on with you? How are you feeling?"

For a moment Skip considered telling Jem about his crippling anxiety and childish fear of the sky, but he couldn't do it. Even when their friendship had been at its strongest, they had never talked about anything serious. They had always been the kind of friends who shared and enjoyed the good times while concealing all evidence of the bad.

"Eh, I'm alright. Things are tough right now, but it's not too bad. I'll get through it," Skip said, waving his hand in dismissal. "What about you? Last I heard you were down in Brooklyn or—"

"Skip," Jem said, interrupting. Drawn by the sudden sharp edge in his friend's voice, Skip finally looked up and

224

met Jem's gaze. It was fierce and unflinching, but not without genuine concern. "Come on. You can tell me what's going on. If you don't want to talk about it, that's fine, but just give me a little something, you know? Tell me how you're holding up. I mean, what happened to you . . . I can't even imagine what that must be like, dealing with the aftermath of that."

"Yeah."

"At least tell me how you're doing. You can do that, right?" Jem said, craning his head to the side and displaying a level of empathy Skip had never seen from him.

"Yeah. I can do that."

"So?"

"Well, if I'm being honest, I'm kind of a mess right now. Ever since I got struck, I've been having a lot of trouble with anxiety related to the weather and storms and stuff like that."

"So what's the problem with that? Millions of people are afraid of storms, even when nothing's happened to them. There's literally nothing wrong with that."

"But I'm—"

"Seriously, you don't have to—"

"I'm afraid of the sky," Skip blurted out. Looking down at the table he felt the heavy slam of his heart, the hot prickle of blood filling his face.

Jem scoffed.

"I still don't see what's so embarrassing about that."

"I don't know, I guess I just feel like I'm going in the wrong direction. I look around and see you and everyone we graduated with, and you're all going out and living on your own and getting married and finding these amazing jobs all over the place, and you all seem so successful and mature. And then here I am, unemployed, still living at home, a brain that's all fucked up, can't even drive a car anymore, afraid of the goddamn sky like a four-year-old. And none of it's going to change. My brain's not going to get much better. The nerve damage in my arm is permanent. And I can barely step outside my front door without having a panic attack. So what the hell can I even do with the rest of my life?"

Jem looked down at the table and shook his head.

"Shit. That's tough. That's really tough, man. I'm really sorry to hear that, but you can't compare yourself to other people like that. I know it's hard, but you got to try to shut all that out and just focus on getting yourself straightened out. You know? And on top of that, it's all bullshit anyway. All of this"—he swept his arm out at his side, gesturing at the bustling room around them—"it's phony. People are just putting up this fake facade of the perfect, idealized version of their life to try to prove how much better they are than everyone else. It's all bullshit. It's just a pissing contest. You can't let yourself get caught up in that," Jem said. Not long after he said this, three guys in their late thirties walked up and asked Jem if they could share the booth. Before Skip could shake his head and say no, Jem nodded and slid in next to Skip. While the three guys sat down across from them, Jem went on talking as if they weren't there. "Now as far as the anxiety goes, let me ask you this. What if it's just a nice, sunny day without any clouds, just a clear blue sky and nothing else? Is that still an issue, or is it just when it's stormy that the anxiety becomes a problem?"

Hearing this, one of the three guys sitting across from them, a guy with a sparse cap of thinning blond hair and a narrow, rectangular face, turned in their direction and studied Skip through squinted eyes.

"That's actually when my anxiety is the highest, since I got struck under a blue sky," Skip said. On his forehead he felt the probing heat of the blond guy's stare, but he forced himself to not look at him.

"Damn. I mean, I know that's a thing that can happen, the whole bolt from the blue shit, but that's absolutely nuts. Because you didn't do anything wrong. It's not like you were running through a thunderstorm with a metal pole in your—"

"I know you!" the blond guy bellowed suddenly, pointing at Skip, his words wet and slurred and messy. "You're supposed to be dead. You're the guy who got struck by lightning and died. I read about you in the paper."

Skip felt his heart starting to slam, the muscles in his legs starting to twitch, so he gestured with his head to Jem as a signal for them to leave.

"Nope, still here. Sorry man," Skip said, following Jem out of the booth.

They left the booth to the three guys and started walking toward the bar. As they slipped through the crowd, Jem turned back to Skip and talked over the noise.

"I've got an idea that might help with some of this anxiety. The only problem is that it involves going outside for a while. Do you think you can do that?"

Behind his eyes Skip felt the hot, blunt throb of an oncoming headache. Though he knew that all the heat and noise of this place would only make it worse, and that going outside was probably the best thing to do, he didn't like the idea. Everything in his head told him he needed more time before he could do that.

"I don't know. I think I'm just going to text my dad and call it a night."

"Okay, how about this. Give me thirty minutes. If we're not in business by then, I'll drive you home myself. Sound good?"

Skip sighed and looked down at the floor. Thinking about what Jem said, Skip realized that putting a finite time limit on the plan was a good idea. Maybe then he'd be able to regulate his anxiety by having a concrete finish line to look forward to.

"I guess, but what are we even talking about here?"

"It's a surprise. But it's good, don't worry. And I think it'll really help with the anxiety you're feeling."

Skip doubted this was the case, but he agreed. This was, after all, why he had forced himself to come here in the first place.

◦──◦

Ten minutes later, while standing in the same spot near the front window where Skip had run into his freshman year lunch buddy an hour earlier, Jem announced that they were in business.

"Ready to go?"

"Where are we going?"

"Outside. The car wash over on Elm. Can you make it there?"

"I don't know, I guess we'll see what happens."

"That's the spirit," Jem said, slapping Skip on the back. "It's going to be worth it. I promise."

They went outside. Just past the door Skip took a quick right to stay underneath the overhang of the building. Waving at Jem to follow, he shuffled past a line of smokers leaning against the wall until he came to an empty spot near the corner. Here he leaned his back against the cold brick, jammed his hands deep in his pockets, and closed his eyes. To calm himself down he took a series of deep breaths. Within each one he felt the icy slice of winter, the acrid sting of cigarette smoke.

"You good?" Jem said.

"Yeah I'm—" Skip said, his anxiety reducing his voice to a thin quiver, "I'm working on it. Just give me a minute."

"There's nothing to be afraid of Skip, we've been over this," a familiar voice said from somewhere on the left. Hearing this voice again, Skip couldn't help but grin. "Your consciousness has already transcended death and the boundary between universes, so what more is there to be afraid of?"

Jem stepped between Skip and his old lunch buddy.

"Thanks man, but he's not feeling too well, so if you could just relax and leave him be, that would be great."

Skip chuckled, opened his eyes, and rested a hand on Jem's shoulder.

"It's alright. We were hanging out before, while I was waiting to meet up with you," Skip said to Jem, the conversation momentarily distracting him from his anxiety. Upon seeing his old lunch buddy's face for a second time tonight, something came loose inside Skip's head, and he suddenly remembered exactly who his old friend was. The name was still gone, but at least now he had a more detailed context in which to place their previous friendship. "We used to sit together at lunch during freshman year and play cards. He's the guy who taught me how to play that Russian card game we used to love."

"Ah yes, *Durak*. Great game," Skip's lunch buddy said. From here he stepped forward, plucked his burning cigarette from his mouth, and offered Jem his hand. He introduced himself as Billy.

"Jeremy," Jem said, shaking Billy's hand. His eyes wandered down to the fanny pack hanging at Billy's hip. "Wait, are you Bill?"

"No. *Bill* is a moderately dickish personal injury lawyer who happens to be my father. If you're ever injured due to someone else's negligence, you go to Bill. For everything else, you come to me," Billy said to Jem. Now he turned his attention to Skip. "But what really matters is this gentleman over here." He pointed at Skip. "We never finished our conversation from before, and I for one have a number of very important questions to ask you about your experience."

Before Skip could say anything, Jem answered for him.

"Sorry man, but we're just about to go meet someone, so we got to get moving if—"

"Well, that works out then, because so am I. I've got a business appointment at an undisclosed location in a few minutes and I don't want to be late," Billy said, dropping his cigarette to the sidewalk and grinding it into the cement with the toe of his fur-lined moccasin. His ankles were very tan, much more so than his face and hands, and he wore no socks. "Shall we go?"

"But you don't even know where we're going," Skip said. Now that he was out here, feeling tiny and exposed and helpless under the massive sky, he wasn't so crazy about the plan anymore. "Didn't you say you have a meeting?"

"Fine, fine," Billy said, turning up the collar of his aviator jacket. He looked at Jem. "Which way are you going? Just point."

Jem shot a quick, inquisitive glance at Skip and then pointed down the street in the direction of Elm and the car wash.

"Good enough. Now," Billy said, throwing a heavy arm around Skip's neck. "About your life in your previous universe."

With these words Billy started walking down the sidewalk in the direction Jem had pointed. Ensnared once again in the grip of his old friend, Skip had no choice but to stumble along for the ride. In seconds he felt his entire body trembling in anticipation of a strike, but ten seconds under the dangerous sky brought nothing. Ten seconds more, and nothing still. And with Billy going off once again about his quantum something-or-other, those seconds soon melted into minutes. Then, before Skip realized what had happened, they were suddenly a block away from the pub, trudging through the cold night, while the creaking, leafless elms loomed above.

Distracted and amused by Billy's monologue, Skip managed to make it all the way to the car wash without his anxiety taking over. Once there, they followed Jem as he walked onto the railroad tracks running alongside the empty building. The wooden cross-planks were thick and old and splintered, and the round stones piled around the tracks kept shifting and clattering underfoot. On the right, Miller's Creek burbled in its bed.

After they had been walking along the tracks in silence for a while, Jem stopped and rested his hands on his sides.

"Hmm. So the guy I was supposed to meet should've been here by now."

Free from Billy's clutches, Skip stared at the creek on the right and tried to think about anything in the world but his memory of those terrible minutes after he got struck. It wasn't working very well, and he could feel his anxiety slowly growing with every idle moment. With these thoughts in mind, he turned to Jem.

"Who are you meeting? What are we even doing here?" Skip said. His lips were cracked and dry and his throat ached from the cold.

"It's for your thing," Jem said, checking his phone. The sharp white light from the screen splashed across his face and dimmed the world behind him. "Don't worry, I still have three minutes left."

"This *is* odd," Billy said from behind. "The other party for my meeting seems to be absent as well."

Hearing this, Jem looked up from his phone, cocked his head to the side, and glared at Billy.

"Dude," Jem said, "you can't be serious."

"I assure you, I am. And my business partner even vouched for this individual before setting up the meeting. Called him a stand-up guy. Very disappointing."

"It's me!" Jem yelled, his voice clapping off the brick wall of the car wash. He jabbed himself in the center of his chest with his fingers. "I'm the guy you're supposed to meet. Jem. I'm Jem, and you're supposed to sell me—"

"Excuse me, sir, but I have near-perfect recall of almost every conversation I've had in the past twenty-five years, and I distinctly remember you telling me that your name is Jeremy, not *Jem*," Billy said, over-enunciating this last word to make it sound as ridiculous as possible. He scoffed, shook his head, and looked to Skip for support.

Skip laughed at this scene and held his hands up in surrender. He was very cold and a little bit dizzy and his bum right arm was trembling badly, but it felt good to be out here in the world like this, breathing the cold air, living some kind of life. It was a universe away from the life he had hoped he'd be living at twenty-five, but it was a hell of a lot better than what he'd been doing for the past five months, cowering in his house in fear.

With his smile lingering on his cold lips, Skip turned back to his friends.

"Okay, okay, whatever, it doesn't matter," Jem said to Billy, pinching the bridge of his nose in exasperation. "Do you have the stuff?"

"I have everything you could ever need, friend. And lucky for you, I don't believe in holding grudges," Billy said, sliding his fanny pack around to the front. "I'll even roll the first one for free, so we can smoke out this little beef of ours."

Following this Jem and Billy shook hands and went about the business of rolling a joint.

After watching this process with curiosity, Skip turned away and looked down at the creek. So it was pot then. That was Jem's big surprise. Though Skip had never tried it before, he still felt a little disappointed. For some reason he'd been expecting something more, something weirder from this new, Serious Adult version of Jem, but apparently the man still had some immaturity left in him. Maybe he wasn't as far gone as Skip had initially feared.

Despite these thoughts, Skip decided to try the pot. He reached out and took the lit joint from Billy's outstretched hand. When he inhaled, the smoke scorched the back of his throat and triggered a honking cough. He handed the thing to Jem and started to walk, following the path laid out by the endless twin rails of the railroad tracks. He had no idea where he was going, and he had no destination in mind, but for the first time in a long while, he wasn't worrying about any of that. All that mattered now was the icy wind in his face, the smoldering itch in his throat, and the two old friends at his side. Everything else could wait until morning.

Huge thanks to Mom and Dad, for the unending support. I love you guys, and without you, this book, and the rest of my writing, would not exist.

Big thanks to Charles and Al for all the support and help in writing and life, and for introducing me to so many cool influences in the worlds of music, movies, books, and games.

Thanks a lot to Baba for all the great stories, the good memories, and the years and years of thoughtful generosity.

Huge thanks to Lucy Zhang for the insightful feedback on almost every one of these stories. Your comments greatly improved the stories in this book, and myself as a writer.

Thanks to Shane Kowolski, Dan Chaon, Ben Niespodziany, and Aaron Burch for writing blurbs for this collection.

Big thanks to David Wojo for designing such a beautiful cover for this book.

Massive thanks to Alan Good for believing in my work, and for turning this book into a reality. I'm incredibly grateful for all your hard work and support.

And thanks to everyone who has ever donated the most valuable resource in the world, time, to read and support my work. That's really damn cool. So thanks for that.

Steve Gergley is the author of *The Great Atlantic Highway & Other Stories* (Malarkey Books '24), *Skyscraper* (West Vine Press '23), and *A Quick Primer on Wallowing in Despair* (Leftover Books '22). His short fiction has appeared or is forthcoming in *X-R-A-Y Literary Magazine*, *Pithead Chapel*, *Maudlin House*, *Passages North*, *Always Crashing*, *Rejection Letters*, and others. In addition to writing fiction, he has composed and recorded five albums of original music. He tweets @GergleySteve. His fiction can be found at: https://stevegergleyauthor.wordpress. com/

Other Titles from Malarkey Books

Faith, a novel by Itoro Bassey
*The Life of the Party Is Harder to Find
Until You're the Last One Around*, poems by Adrian Sobol
Music Is Over, a novel by Ben Arzate
Toadstones, stories by Eric Williams
Deliver Thy Pigs, a novel by Joey Hedger
It Came From the Swamp, edited by Joey Poole
Pontoon, an anthology of fiction and poetry
What I Thought of Ain't Funny,
edited by Caroljean Gavin
Guess What's Different, essays by Susan Triemert
White People on Vacation, a novel by Alex Miller
Your Favorite Poet, poems by Leigh Chadwick,
Sophomore Slump, poems by Leigh Chadwick
Man in a Cage, a novel by Patrick Nevins
Fearless, a novel by Benjamin Warner
Don Bronco's (Working Title) Shell, a novel?
by Donald Ryan
Un-ruined, a novel by Roger Vaillancourt
Thunder From a Clear Blue Sky,
a novel by Justin Bryant
Kill Radio, a novel by Lauren Bolger

The Muu-Antiques, a novel by Shome Dasgupta
Backmask, a novel by OF Cieri
Gloria Patri, a novel by Austin Ross
Where the Pavement Turns to Sand,
stories by Sheldon Birnie
Still Alive, a novel by LJ Pemberton
Hope and Wild Panic, stories by Sean Ennis
Sleep Decades, stories by Israel A. Bonilla
I Blame Myself But Also You (and Other Stories),
by Spencer Fleury
Thumbsucker, poems by Kat Giordano
First Aid for Choking Victims,
stories by Matthew Zanoni Müller

DEATH OF PRINT TITLES

Consumption & Other Vices, a novel by Tyler Dempsey
Awful People, a novel by Scott Mitchel May
Drift, a novel by Craig Rodgers
The Ghost of Mile 43, a novel by Craig Rodgers
One More Number, stories by Craig Rodgers
Francis Top's Grand Design, stories by Craig Rodgers
Francis Top's Lost Cipher, stories by Craig Rodgers

Milton Keynes UK
Ingram Content Group UK Ltd.
UKHW011448050524
442175UK00004B/188

9 798990 324091